Tame Me Fiercely

FLIPPED FAIRYTALES

ZIA TYREE

To my perfect husband for showing me a love that most would travel an ocean to find.

Flipped Fairytales

Tame Me Fiercely *Zia Tyree*

Wish Me Freely *Aly Hollis*

Rob Me Blindly *Harlowe Savage*

Drown Me Gently *Tereza Kane*

Freeze Me Slowly *Abigail Schmitz*

Carry Me Sweetly *Laney Arden*

Deal Me Darkly *Jade Nioma*

Claim Me Fearlessly *Alexis Almanzar*

Bury Me Endlessly *Kay Lalock*

Free Me Truly *Cara Blaine*

More coming soon...

Chapter 1

22 years ago...

"Nathaniel! I don't know how much longer I can hold on!" Emilia shouted with faltering breath over the rushing waters. She was soaked to the bone, shivering from adrenaline and drenched garments. Emilia's left arm was going numb clutching their newborn babe, the other gripped the seat nearest her husband who remained steady at the helm. The unexpected rainstorm crashed over the ship, unrelenting in its wake.

"Just a little longer, my love! You can do this!" Nathaniel's steadfast confidence attempted to get them as close as possible to the shore. He desperately hoped they could swim the rest of the way before the vessel sank. The young couple and their babe were the only ones left on the ship. Its original captain and crew were tossed off in the storm's original assault a mere thirty minutes before.

The choppy waters threw every grown, seasoned man a part of their crew off the ship as if they were under attack by Neptune himself. The vessel they took was smaller than usual, and with a smaller crew. But this was supposed to support a shorter mission during this season. It was never supposed to be like this. Nathaniel was sure the water claimed the men's lives in the way their vows had always known they would be taken. Davy Jones fed on souls, each as a token for another's safe passage. But it wouldn't take his family. Emilia and Thea would live.

"I see it! I see it! Oh, god, Nathaniel, I see trees," Emilia screeched, her throat ragged from pleading with whatever god would listen. Little Thea joined her mother in emoting, crying and wriggling through the wrap she had been swaddled in.

This was in no way how they intended on visiting the small, luxurious island, yet to be named. The couple, now in their early thirties, had spent the last decade of life exploring unknown terrain employed by the Crown. Their home country demanded ownership on lands others were not yet aware of. Nathaniel and Emilia were steady in their service to the Crown, this was supposed to be the last installment of exploration before they started the next chapter of their work at the University.

After meeting on their first voyage to a desert acropolis, it was love at first sight. Emilia sketched the animals and foliage throughout their various journeys, eager to link species to currently known taxonomy. Nathaniel was adept at studying animal behavior. He pursued the belief that all life forms were intelligent, thinking creatures to various degrees. Emilia insisted this voyage would be a good thing for the whole family. Her pregnancy had made her too nauseous to tolerate any travel by boat last year, and she believed early exposure to wildlife would instill curiosity in their daughter.

"Do you see that up ahead?" Nathaniel shouted while his broad shoulders struggled against the counterforce against the wheel. Lightning struck one of the trees visible on the shore. The leaves burst into flames, a hellscape unfolding before them. Death by sea or death by land. Emilia began to disassociate, wondering which would be the least pleasurable.

"Yes! Yes, I do! Is the life raft still intact?" Emilia asked her husband. She felt her backpack full of their most precious belongings and survival tools as the only weight against her soaking body.

"No, it ripped off a few minutes ago!" Nathaniel tossed a look to the side where Emilia couldn't see. "I thought the Queen ordered a sturdier boat! What the hell is this?"

Emilia spared a moment to wipe water from her brow, attempting to get a clearer visual of what lay before them. Her deep brunette hair was gratefully in a braid down her back, but the bangs slicked across her forehead barely gave way.

"We'll have to swim the rest of the way! Are there any jackets or rafts on the craft that you saw?" Emilia whipped her head around the damaged ship, stretching to see any possibility of escape. She should have done her own safety inspection instead of relying on the crew this time around. There was simply too much to think about at once as a new mother.

"No," Nathaniel said, bile rising in his throat. He quickly looked between the love of his life, still so devastatingly beautiful among the mess, and their perfect, small creature. He would never have enough time to decode the structure of love he held for his family. "Emilia, I-"

And just then, a surge of water overcame what was left of the vessel.

CHAPTER 2

10 years ago...

"And that, my love, is how we found ourselves here," Emilia searched Thea's deep green eyes, matching her father's. Mother and daughter were safe, nuzzled under the canopy in their makeshift home. Stars threatened to peek inside. Emilia made note of reinforcing the edges of their enclosure, worried about the heavy rain season about to come upon them.

"You always say Father was very strong and brave," Thea's sleepy voice crooned into a yawn, and she stretched her arms up and above her head. Even at the age of twelve, she fought sleep, wanting to hear story after story about a man she would never meet, and cities she would never visit. "I wish he was still with us. He sounds... wonderful."

"More than you could ever know," Emilia suppressed welling tears. "His job was to get you and I here to safety, and that's exactly what he did. My job was to take over the rest. Now you and I are here until..." Her voice trailed off, unsure of where to go next. She had told the story in various iterations over the years, and yet it hurt every time. Emilia ran through her daughter's thick, dark hair, pushing it back to make space to kiss her soft forehead.

"Until when, Mother? Will the Queen come and get us? I hope not. I like playing with my friends." Thea pulled the makeshift blanket up to her chin, nuzzling in for the night.

"Well, I still believe that perhaps our human friends are looking for us. In the meantime, you get to be in school with your mum. You know, I am a professor, after all," Emilia huffed out a small laugh. "Sleep now, Wild One. I'll tell you more about how we honeymooned in a place similar to this in the morning."

Soft snores were her only response. When they grew more even and deep, Emilia shifted her weight on their shared cot, and slid out from underneath the young girl. She looked at her daughter, inspecting every inch of her growing face. They might have been talking about growing pains and menstrual cycles over the past few weeks, but when she was asleep, Emilia could still picture her at each age. Coming of age was a difficult conversation for any woman, so Emilia approached every sensitive topic through the simple lens of biology and science. She could only pray to the gods she no longer believed in that she was raising her daughter right.

Perhaps when Thea was older and stronger they could craft a boat together and sail back home safely.

She opened the flap of the makeshift chambers, and Emilia yearned for a real bed for the first time in a long time. She shrugged, and twisted and turned every which way. She ran her fingers through unruly hair, wishing for a stronger brush and sturdier twine to keep it up and out of her face. Her body was stiff from compiling the latest bits of wreckage that landed upon the shore. On occasion, driftwood and rope helped her to expand their abode. In fact, shortly after she awoke on the new island, vestiges from their own ship came to the shore with some pieces of luggage and a scant variety of tools to assist her. The smallest blessing she was offered in her new, cruel reality.

Above all, she believed they would be rescued. Surely, they weren't forgotten. Her Queen would never turn her back on them. Not after so many years of discovery and service.

Every evening, she would walk the grounds to prepare fruit for the next day's breakfast, still ever cautious of what botanicals could harm them. She was met with heavy, frustrated grunting.

"Well, hello, Mala," Emilia said to the massive, hulking female gorilla pacing around her home. "She's asleep, finally, so keep it quiet, will you?"

Mala huffed in response, and Emilia found it comforting. Ever since she crashed onto the island ten years ago, she made a severe effort to bond to the hoard of gorillas, working with them in every way Nathaniel would have wanted.

"You're rather territorial this evening. Everything all right?" Emilia signed alongside her speech toward the female primate. Her daughter rarely had to sign to the animals. Ever since Thea developed speech, they listened. It was almost eerie the way they seemed to understand the lesser-developed language of a human child. The females in her tribe were incredibly helpful, maternal even. Their strength was intimidating, but they were gentle creatures beyond this.

Mala pulled Emilia and Thea from the wreckage those years ago, as she was nearly unconscious. She named the gorilla after a friend she and Nathaniel had met in the early years of adventure, a band-aid around her heart just to say the name and after the kindness she was bestowed. Thea was just a baby then, floating on her belly barely above the water.

Emilia found a piece of driftwood to cling to, but that was the last of her memories around the event. Emilia shivered at the thought of what might have happened without the gorilla's generosity and instinct. The two females created an inexplicable bond, learning each other's habits and culture.

Just as Emilia taught little Thea the universal human language and sign language, she also taught the gorillas how to communicate. First through sign language, then with verbal cues that worked its way to fragmented human language. No creature dared come close to Emilia and Thea as long as Mala was around. Emilia suspected Mala had suffered a loss of her own infant with the tender care she demonstrated toward Thea. Her arms could rip them apart in seconds, but the sounds of infant to toddler to little girl never startled Mala.

Once, just a year prior, Thea asked Mala to pick her up and take her into the trees. Mala complied after Emilia gave a curt nod. It was as if... no. Emilia shook her head at the preposterous thought.

The gorilla never answered Emilia's inquiry, but that wasn't unusual if there were predators around. Emilia's skin prickled with the awareness that something was watching them.

A rustling through the forest made Emilia's head snap. Mala looked to follow her gaze, and just as Emilia started to back away from the sound, a massive, slinky creature pounced from the brush.

A scream that was so fierce shook the forest floor.

It tore the underbrush apart.

"Mala! Save her! Go! Go now!" Emilia fought and distracted the puma, searching for something, anything on the ground. Mala rushed to her aide, but the puma's tail snapped her along the face, disorienting the gorilla. Mala stumbled back and toward the hut where Thea lay sleeping. The puma's hot breath bore down over Emilia, saliva dripping into her eyes. Emilia kicked so hard, she broke free momentarily, barely able to secure a large rock in her hand. A fierceness Emilia had never known overtook herself, as she smashed the rock against the animal's head. In the same instant, it sunk its teeth into her neck.

"Nathaniel... I'm sorry," Emilia gasped, her lover's name still clinging to her lips.

The last thing she saw as she and the puma lay dying on the forest floor was Thea clinging to Mala's back, winding through the vines.

CHAPTER 3

Present Day

"Come now, you're much too fast!" Thea felt the wind whipping through her long, unruly locks as she swung from vine to vine, laughing all the way. She was covered in scraps of cloth, one bandage around her top, and ratty old shorts covering her bottom.

She smiled wide all the way home, jumping down from the last vine and plopping right in front of her chosen mother. She always bent her knees to lessen the impact of the landing, and this time was no different. Thea kicked up a little dirt just for fun.

Mala raised a large hand in greeting, huffing out her discontentment.

In put-up nonchalance, Thea pushed her tangled hair out of her face, as if she wasn't sweating for a moment. She hadn't seen herself in a mirror that wasn't a reflection in the water, and her understanding of self was only pieced together in the memories of her mother, but she couldn't have looked that bad. She smelled her armpits. Nothing too atrocious.

"We were just having fun! No need to be upset." Thea grabbed the large gorilla's head and planted a kiss atop it, like her mother used to do to her. She was only twelve years old when she was killed, but there was so much Thea committed to memory. The most important of them all was the way her mom made her feel. Thea received an incredible education in a short amount of time, "in case of an emergency," her mother used to say. She recalled much of what happened to be an emergency and she was grateful for Mala's care because of it.

A larger gorilla stepped out from the side, with several infants following him.

"What did you do?" the Boss signed, clearly frustrated in his own way with Thea.

"I was swinging," she started to move her body around and around, flinging herself until she was dizzy, "and then I got caught up in a pack," she signed again.

She wasn't just romping around with her gorilla friends, swinging around the forest. She was increasingly disturbing communities around them. She yearned to explore, to learn more. Thea explored the entire island at this point, and was starting to grow weary of the repetitive nature of her days. By Thea's calculations, she was twenty two years old. Although, she wasn't sure at what age her gorilla family expected her to be grown at. She stopped growing in height at around fourteen. So annoying.

When it was safe to return to her home after the puma attack, Thea looked upon the tiny cot and stacks of leaves with ink on them, and tried to decode their messages. But she couldn't. Mala had found her sobbing among everything. She wanted to understand her mother's journaling, but wasn't old enough to grasp most of the concepts, many of them using scientific language she hadn't yet learned. The ink and paper her mother made, though resourceful, had become water-dredged. Her mother's reinforcements didn't hold up as anticipated.

Mala guided her to a pile of rocks signing "mother" and "love". Mala pointed first to the ground, then to herself, and finally to the area she and her mother lived in. The sound of her mother's screams came rushing back, and hot tears threatened to drown her entirely.

Hush now, child. Everything is alright.

There was a soothing voice in her head. Looking back, it must have been a long-forgotten memory, a child's mind creating one homogenous version of a mother figure for comfort. How strange.

The only remnant of her mother she could understand was the never-ending drawings produced, drawn with what materials she had or created on pulp paper her mother derived from crushed, dried leaves and water. She also took back sketches of herself when she was small and sketches of who she assumed was her father. A portrait of them as a family she kept under her pillow in her new home with the gorillas. Thea wasn't sure that she'd ever return to the site of the crime again.

Her latest effort in self-education was the population of elephants- how they moved, how they interacted with one another. It was one of the few species she repeatedly encountered with little to no success. She peered at them near a body of water, and attempted to mimic their sound. She didn't come close. At all.

This day, their large ears and tusks turned toward her.

"What's so hard to understand? I'm Thea! Nice to meet you!" She threw out her arms, making herself as large as possible.

And then they charged. She barely made it out alive, and clearly, word traveled fast.

"Surprised you're alive," the Boss signed back, chuffing loudly enough to startle the infants around him. His stern nature was derived from being their leader and her de facto father figure. He just wanted everyone safe.

The forest around them was clean, beautiful, and undisturbed. She liked it that way. Thea felt like she wasn't alone, but still wanted more. She worried if she didn't show appreciation now for her father, she'd be seen as ungrateful.

So, as she had from when she was little, she wrapped her entire body around his leg, laughing when it was harder than usual for him to pick her up. But not impossible.

She made soothing chuffs and grunting noises, hoping he would forgive her. She had a curious nature and there was nearly nothing her adoptive parents could do about it. Thea picked at the large gorilla's fur, watching him wince with each tuft tugged on.

Ouch!

She heard a gruff male voice in her head. She jumped back from the Boss. He cocked his head at her. Hearing an inner voice outside of her own was incredibly disturbing. The older she got, the more frequently it occurred. She never knew her father, but she thought she heard her mother at least once before.

What was this?

"Did you just say 'Ouch'?" Asking out loud felt a bit incredulous, but here she was.

The Boss simply turned around.

"Hey! You come back here!" Thea ran on all fours after him. "I know I'm not the most skilled cleaner, but helping tend to this family is what I do best!"

She knew his frustrations lay in the fact that the troop could be disrupted because of her angst and her inability to keep to herself. Her conversations were nearly always one-sided.

Her... humanness was a threat to their existence the longer she was around. But what else was she supposed to do? Where was she to go?

He finally laughed in his own way, and tossed her on his back, running in a circle as everyone beat their chests. Thea knew he wouldn't be able to be mad at her for too long.

"Slow down," Mala signed and punctuated by stomping the ground.

The Boss listened to his mate, and Thea softly wondered if she needed that type of love. She had the love of her primate family, and the jungle seemed to listen to her. In the end, she decided she did.

Zia Tyree

CHAPTER 4

Thea awoke the next morning to a deafening crack. She rubbed her eyes quickly, wondering if it was a remnant of the nightmare she was having. The nightmares started when her mom left, and they invaded her sleep from time to time.

She shed her makeshift blanket to find her skin damp. The weather was temperate, so she had been sweating through the night.

Another crack rang out. Definitely not a nightmare, then.

She jumped to open the leafy door to her hut. She looked to her left and right, attempting to trace where the sound came from with sleepy eyes and tangled hair. She pushed the strands out of her eyes, orienting herself to the bright morning and chaos before her. Below her, down the hill, lived the rest of her family. They were also awake and scrambling while the second crack rang out. Birds soared above, disrupting leaves and branches in their wake. Thea covered her ears and yelled for her family below as she ran toward them.

The Boss pointed in the general direction that he thought the sound came from. He meant her to join them in running away from it. She locked eyes with him.

GO! NOW!

In a split second, she realized. He had been speaking to her not just through sign language. But in her thoughts. So had Mala. So had some of the other pack members. This simply couldn't be normal. But she didn't have a choice.

Mala screeched after her to stop, but Thea ran. She pumped her legs hard and fast scrambling up the moss-covered tree, searching for purchase with each foot she gained. Mala beat her strong fists at the trunk of the tree, nearly rattling Thea free. But it was no use. The Boss pulled Mala away, kicking and screaming in her own way, leading her away from Thea and the choice she made to abandon them to investigate the sound.

If someone came to harm her family, they'd soon learn their lesson. She assumed she was average height for a woman, filling out the clothes her mother had left behind. With much more muscle tone. She could put up a fight if needed.

Thea jumped from the tree she climbed up, and swung vine to vine, heading straight where the Boss gestured. Her upper back ached from the strain, as she never got a chance to stretch after the events of yesterday. Nor did she get to eat any breakfast before taking off. Or take her morning bath. Now was not the time to worry about her aching stomach or how she smelled. Perhaps that would make her all the more off-putting to intruders.

So much had been taken from Thea, images of her mother whipping past her faster than what she could see in front of her face. When she was frightened, her mother's voice came to her like a ghost and this time was no different.

Slow down, Wild One. You might hurt yourself.

She only went faster.

Be with Mala and the Boss. They will protect you.

Later. She would find them again. *Hear* them again. For now, she realized she was headed toward where the sand and the water met.

Turn back. TURN BACK NOW.

She had to see the commotion for herself. Her mother spoke of terrifying stories of humans who were not like herself and her father. People who would see her home and her family destroyed and dissected. In Thea's mind, they were all the same. All connected. All one family. Or could they be of the same mind? Did others possess her love of nature and the creatures that inhabit her home? There was only one way to find out.

Perhaps fifteen minutes later, Thea swung up to the last tree she could feasibly get to. Sweat dripped down her back, and her palms were slick. The spike of adrenaline tore her up from the inside, and she did everything in her power to quiet her breathing. She was the predator looking among some potential prey. She must act accordingly.

Thea needed a vantage point to observe those who dared to encroach upon her territory. With a sharpened gaze and cocked ears, Thea leaned over a branch to listen to the conversation around her. Her strong legs kept her position locked, and she already tested the tensile strength of the branch before crawling out over it.

It had been ten years since she heard another human speak. A decade since she looked upon a face that was so close to her own, it hurt. It was foreign. She rarely produced full sentences with the gorillas, anymore. Her speech hadn't grown too far past what her mother taught her, but she knew that her emotions and capacity for understanding had grown up with her.

There was a large ship out on the water, sitting still and unmoving. Smoke billowed out from the middle of it. Thea wondered how much wood it took to create that much fire and smoke. She scanned the rippling water that emanated from the ship, leading to a smaller rowboat holding three people down on the sand.

"AHOY! Anyone around?" A large broad man was at the helm of the rowboat, with two others rowing behind him. He appeared to be much older than Thea, gray hairs intermingling with a dark blond slick-back style. She tried to not be afraid of his presence. He was the first man she'd ever seen.

CRACK.

Another flare left the device in his hands, and launched into the air. Thea ducked her head reactively at the sound, much louder now that she was closer to the source. The red sparks went everywhere, and the surprise of it nearly made Thea lose her grip. She steadied herself and tuned in again.

"Stop that this instant, Mr. Ridgewell! I nearly lost my grip on this oar." The woman in the middle of the boat was petite, with gray hair barely kept in a ponytail at her nape. She wore a buttoned up blouse, high-waisted trousers, and what appeared to be sensible shoes.

"Nonsense, Aggie. This will ensure no beast gets closer than we want them to."

"It's Dr. Perch to you, you big buffoon!" She yelled with a huff.

She blew at her gray curls to push them out of her face. Thea smiled. She liked this woman.

Thea looked back at her own feet.

Shoes.

Thea couldn't remember having such proper shoes. Her mom put together what she called a "sandal" for padding around the forest floor. Thea, on the other hand, believed in touching the earth around her, wanting to become one with it. She built up callouses as she got older on her hands and feet, making it easier to grip the bark and vines she clung to for transportation. Her feet were fine enough, she assured herself.

Thea scrunched her brow once more to catch a glimpse of the second male figure in the boat.

The man was tall as well, but not as broad. He was glistening from the sun, light brown hair laid against his forehead. He was shaking his head, looking ahead with determined concentration. He worked the oars with long sleeves rolled up to the elbow. He wore tan pants that stretched taught from each push. Her breath caught at his physique. So different from hers, that must be where her fascination lay. She needed to get closer. To speak with them. But she wasn't sure how.

The smaller boat was docked on the shore, and the man in the back held out his hand to the older woman. She couldn't believe the man in front when he just hopped off the boat and didn't do a thing to help either of his travel companions. His arrogance was already wearing on her. If both of the men were like this, she might never bother approaching.

"Thank you, dear," the woman named Aggie said, "At least someone has manners around here."

"Of course, mum, watch your step. Let me grab your bag," the younger man said.

She watched him closely as he leaned toward the back of the rowboat. His shirt pulled north, and she caught a glimpse at the expanse of his back.

"Thank you, sweetheart. Now let's be careful as we approach. The last venture here did not make it back. We're lucky the Queen wanted us here again—" She was cut off.

"Yes, mum. We're very lucky. Do you have everything you need in your satchel?"

The older woman rummaged through the bag until she pulled out a large brimmed hat and plunked it on her head. "Yes! I believe I do."

The younger man reached once again to the back of the boat and unbolted a large package. He seemed to be a similar age to Thea.

"Let's find a spot to set up camp. We have about six hours before sundown, and we wouldn't want to be caught in the dark without a place to sleep."

"Yes, go ahead and do that. I think I'll go hunting for some food," the older man said with a dark smile.

Thea hadn't noticed the thick strap across the older man's chest that was attached to a long metal object. This looked like a weapon her mother warned her of, although she was not sure what its specific purpose was. Thea's only weapons were long blades she fashioned out trees and sharper objects to spear fish or to ward off predators. The length of the metal appeared like a reed, with no point to the end, so at least he couldn't spear her with it.

"We have some stores already. We won't need much else for a few days. There's no need to kill anything when all we have to do is signal the ship to get them to ferry more supplies." The younger man had a biting tone when it came to the older one. Adversaries, but forced here together? Curious.

"Who cares about stores when we could have something fresh for tonight?"

"You're going to drive off any chance we might have with the gorillas," the younger man said sternly. "That gun goes off, and we'll have to circle to the other side of the island. You'll waste time. Again!"

"Come now, let's work together to set up our tents. We're here for a reason!" The older woman got in between the two men holding her hands out and redirecting their attention.

"I'm going to explore a bit. I won't kill anything," the older man grumbled. "Yet."

Only Thea could hear the last part. Her heart began to pick up speed again. They were here to... study... her family. But it looked as though one member appeared more nefarious than the other two.

The older man was clearly not the younger man's father. She would never think to speak up against her elders in that tone. Gorillas were nothing if not polite. Even though that was exactly what she was about to do.

It seemed as though her only option was to get in front of this while she could.

Thea's long legs aided her soundless repelling down the tree, and her feet were instantly warm on the sand. She didn't find herself on the outskirts of the island often, as she preferred the soft brush of grass underneath her feet to the harshness of the sand. Unless you were close to the water, the direct sun was almost too much to bear most days.

Thea debated whether or not she should stick around to watch the mother and son for a moment, but she realized the hesitation would cost her. Instead, she picked up a nearby stick with the sharpest edge she could find, and stalked the large man through the overgrowth he passed through.

Five minutes had gone by, and she still hadn't caught sight of the man. She crept around trees waiting for him to make a noise, signaling his direction. Just when she thought perhaps he had turned around, she was shoved face-first into the wet ground in front of her. Blood dripped out of her nose as she turned around to catch her attacker.

"And what do we have here? Are you here alone or are there others?" The man whipped his head in either direction, apparently awaiting an onslaught. His breathing slowed as he realized that she was the only one around.

The stick was still pressed firmly into her palm, but she had to be smart about her tactics. She wiped the blood from her nose without saying a word. He was wearing a weapon on his back, and he was larger than her. Speed and agility were her only advantages against a man so tall. She dimly wondered if this is what her father had looked like in any capacity. If this man had a daughter, it didn't seem much like it at all.

Thea grunted and sat upright, slowly, assessing her surroundings. Three nearby trees, no vines swayed around her to quickly grab onto and the trunks were too large to climb up quickly. She didn't want to give away that she could speak just yet. Being a feral creature had few advantages.

The man circled her.

"You're not going to get as far as you think. I'm just not sure what you're planning to do with that... stick." He gestured at her feeble weapon, not knowing her game plan.

Good.

That was all she needed. A moment of confusion for her to strike.

She lunged with a roar, ricocheting off of a rock near her.

She came down on the man hard, throwing her elbow into his temple. He staggered, and she used the leverage to climb onto his back, wrapping her strong legs around his front. Her heels pushed into his gut, and he lurched forward. Thea brought the large stick in front of his throat, effectively cutting off his airway. He attempted to bring what she now recognized as a gun toward her, but she redirected it toward the sky.

The other humans weren't too far away it seemed, and they ran through the foliage to catch up to Thea and her assailant.

"What the hell is going on here, Mr. Ridgewell?" Thea caught a glimpse of the younger man as she wrestled this Ridgewell creature to the ground.

"She! Attacked! Me!" Mr. Ridgewell could barely get out a word, and she wondered how long he could go without breathing. Perhaps not much longer.

"Hi, dear. Do you mind letting go of this man?" The petite elderly woman didn't seem particularly attached to him, so Thea found this strange. "We would also like to strangle him on the occasion, but he's helping us run this expedition. Jonathan, would you mind helping this young woman get herself settled once she releases our unfortunate colleague?"

Now that made more sense.

Despite her better judgement, Thea loosened her grip only slightly. She tossed a look to the beautiful man named Jonathan, needing another point of reassurance. He had incredibly kind, brown eyes. They looked like the warm bark that protected her favorite trees. He fit in so seamlessly, so quickly.

The names felt weird floating around in her head. It had been so long since she had heard new names. Also, strangle. That must have been the action that she was taking now.

Jonathan put both large hands in front of him, much like she did to larger animals to appease them. He lowered one knee to the ground to reach eye-level with her.

"Hi," he murmured, a little breathless. She was uncertain if he was afraid of her. She didn't want him to be afraid. She wanted him to like her? Maybe as a new friend, or maybe more. "Do you speak English?"

She waited a beat before nodding her head yes.

"Okay, I see we got off on the wrong foot." He flashed a brilliant, warm smile. "I'm John. Or Jonathan. Whichever you prefer."

One interaction with this man and all of her best, most self-preserving ideas left her mind. She reluctantly let Mr. Ridgewell go. She rolled backwards and away from the group of newcomers to keep some distance in case she needed to flee in a hurry. Mr. Ridgewell panted and wheezed, clutching his throat.

"You fucking bitch!"

Jonathan reacted so quickly, she was sure her eyes were deceiving her. Jonathan pushed him back down to the ground, and stood larger than life above him.

He whispered with a deadly calm, "We are in the presence of a lady. Fucking act like it. Or we'll abandon this project. You'll have to tell the Queen how you assaulted a woman no less than an hour after docking. So what's it going to be, Chase?"

Thea unknowingly walked toward Jonathan's mother. Gravitating toward the first human woman she'd seen in ten years felt natural. Both women worried over the situation before them. Her poor heart beat out of her chest, and she wasn't sure how to get it to stop.

"Fine. I'll stop. For now." Mr. Ridgewell, whose first name must be Chase, sputtered out.

"Do you have a name? You must be terribly frightened," John said soothingly as he turned, looking Thea over, his full mouth slightly parted.

CHAPTER 5

A name. Thea had never been asked her name before. At least, not in so many words. Her throat was scratchy from breathing so hard, and she wasn't sure she could form the words.

"Thea," she said finally.

"Thea," John responded reverently. "That's beautiful. Do you have a last name? And are you injured anywhere?"

He took a step forward, and she took a step back. She hadn't prepared for him to advance, but he kept striding forward. He paused.

A last name. Like they each had possessed.

"Not that I know of. And I'm okay," she said with mild embarrassment. Her mother made mention of a last name at some point, she was sure. But what good was a last name without a human family to back it up with? Legacy was low on her list of survival-related priorities.

"That's quite alright," he chanced another step in her direction. Not to make contact it seemed, but as though being generally near her was the only thing his body would allow him to do.

"It's alright. I'd just like to shake your hand," John smiled reassuringly.

"Shake your hand?" Thea questioned.

He lifted his palm toward hers, signaling that he was just using one hand. This would be easier than having other animals sniff her rear end. Quieter than birds chirping amongst themselves.

She met his palm in the air, moving their hands up and down together, wondering if this is how you'd shake a hand. The contact stole her breath, and she was curious to know if it was like this with every other human encounter, or if it was the novelty that stunned her.

He chuckled softly, and she felt her cheeks go red. This was not going well. She pulled away and he caught her wrist gently.

"Here. Let me show you." John wrapped his hand around her own, encasing it in the most delicate warmth she had ever felt. When they locked eyes as he moved their hands in proper synchrony, she felt a similar warmth grow in her chest. The easiest fire she'd ever started, and it came from within.

"Let me show *you*!" Thea smiled brightly, shaking vigorously.

"Oh, what a delight!" Dr. Perch clapped her hands lightly together, looking between the two of them. "Now tell us, darling girl, who else are you here with?"

"I am with the animals." Thea looked around herself to see if any companions had followed or if they continued steering clear of the danger. No one was around, and she figured it was for the best.

"They are elsewhere, as a result of the commotion." Thea leveled a glare at Mr. Ridgewell.

"Are there others like you? On this island?" Jonathan asked, looking into the same forest she was just peeking through.

She looked between his mother and Mr. Ridgewell, cautiously lowering her weapon for the sake of conversation. "No, I'm the only one left. My mother..." she trailed off unsure of how to answer. Her mother had been gone a long time but she was the only one she'd ever known or effectively conversed with. "She's dead. She's been dead for ten years," she said plainly.

"Oh, my dear. I am so terribly sorry to hear that. I know your mother must be so proud of the woman you've become. Surviving so many years alone," Dr. Perch tsked lightly, and looked to her son with a hint of sadness.

Thea set her shoulders, proud of having taken care of herself for so long.

"Again, I'm okay. As you can see." She gestured down her body, hoping to relieve the tension in the air. She was physically fit, after all.

"So, these animals, you say. Where are they?" Mr. Ridgewell finally pushed himself to his feet. He reached out his hand to shake as well, but Thea retreated a step. She didn't want to touch Mr. Chase Ridgewell again. Ever. Jonathan, on the other hand...

Jonathan moved into a protective position in front of her.

"How about we start with the basics, Mr. Ridgewell," Jonathan said, apparently going back to formalities. "Thea- My mother is Dr. Perch."

"You can call me Aggie. He can't though." She gestured with her thumb where Mr. Ridgewell stood.

"Aggie," she said, feeling it on her tongue. It was fun to say. "Aggie, Aggie, Aggie!" she said with a smile.

"Yes! Aggie! Very well. Why don't you show us around? We don't need to meet your chosen family just yet. We'll be on the island for two weeks."

Chosen family was what she realized she had called them as well. Motherly understanding was transcendent. They communicated almost as easily as her and her mother did when she was little. If anything, they chose her, letting her into their homes and feeding her and helping clothe her.

Also, Thea knew weeks were made up of seven days a piece, but Thea only tracked time in years at this point, continuing tally marks her mother left behind on a giant slab of stone. Three hundred and sixty five of them made up most years. So that's how she knew.

"You saw the bank of sand, what else are you here to see?" Thea questioned.

"We're here to study the plants and the nature around you. The queen has commissioned us to document the happenings of the island to see if it's worthwhile," Jonathan said.

"What does 'worthwhile' mean? To you?" Thea gestured to the group. She avoided her heart skipping a beat at mention of the queen. What was so worth studying right now? She could tell them anything they wanted to know. And then they should leave.

"Well, right now, we're researching how animals interact in different environments and with different stressors. I'd love to hear more about your story and how you fit into their dynamic," Dr. Perch answered excitedly.

"Okay. I can answer those questions. I don't know if I'll let you around my family, though." Thea began to take up a defensive posture, suddenly finding herself encircled by the group.

Jonathan sensed her distrust and pushed Mr. Ridgewell back with a steady hand.

"How about we start with some food? I'm starving," Jonathan smiled easily at her. Her heart stilled for a moment, feeling like she would recognize that smile anywhere, despite never seeing a man in her life.

Chapter 6

About an hour later, Thea had set up something of an eating station on the sandy beach. She could see the absolutely massive parent ship that was docked some distance away. Jonathan explained that the bank wasn't suitable to dock a ship that size right up on the beach, meaning they would have to take trips back and forth to the main boat. She nodded her understanding, although she wasn't quite certain on its mechanics. The sun was out for lunchtime, but Thea found a copse of trees for the group to get a reprieve from.

She retrieved a stick, whittled it into a point strong enough to break through a coconut, and used another branch for leverage to crack it open, slurping down the contents. She could feel her lips drying, a clear sign she needed nutrition and hydration. She used her system to crack a few more, giving them to her newfound guests. Well, the Perches. Mr. Ridgewell was on his own before he dehydrated himself. He stalked off to find his own coconut, leaving her alone with the mother and son.

She wasn't entirely sure how to feed anyone beside herself. The other animals are so self-sufficient. She hoped the group of scholars would have some of their own sustenance. Although it wouldn't be as fresh as the fish she caught.

"If you're hungry, umm, can I help you fish? I don't know what you eat," Thea looked between them.

"Oh dear, the coconut is just lovely! You don't need to feed us, we have a supplier that runs food and other materials back and forth from the ship." Dr. Perch gestured toward the large ship not too far off the coast.

As she was speaking, another small boat was approaching the shore. It carried more crates than men.

"Speak of the devil, Mason is here with our first round of equipment. How about I leave you to start your own... research?" Dr. Perch winked at her son conspiratorially.

Thea leaned into Jonathan. Wow, he smelled incredible. Like sweat and something earthy she couldn't place. Could this be his natural scent or an oil he used to make himself more attracted to mates?

"What is... the devil? Did that have something to do with your religion?" Thea's mother was a pragmatist who only prayed when she thought Thea was asleep. The devil could mean multitudes to different people, so again, she was unsure. Thea squinted at the doctor, trying to figure out what was in the crates, as if she could see right through the wood.

"It's more of a phrase we use. I'm a scientist, not a man of god." Jonathan chuckled. "But as the seconds with you tick by I could be convinced of something greater. Your survival must have been no small feat," John said confidently.

"How long did it take you to get here? And how quickly can you go back?" Thea asked. She didn't want to speak on her survival. She only wanted to learn as much as she could about the outside world.

"So eager to get rid of me so soon, Wild One?"

Thea glitched. Her whole body stuttered in the spot she sat cross legged. A shred of coconut meat fell out of her mouth and into her lap. She picked it up without worrying over appearances. No food could go to waste.

"What did you just say?" Thea flushed.

"I was only poking fun. We're here for two weeks, and then we'll be out of your hair. Unless, you change your mind about where home is." He looked at her almost hopefully.

"No, not that. I understand you'll be leaving soon," she said, disregarding the idea that she would ever leave the only home she's ever known. "What you called me."

"Wild One? I'm not sure why, it just came to me. You're in a jungle, with your beautiful hair every which way. I love how independent and wild you've been on your own. It's impressive, to say the least." Jonathan picked out another piece of coconut meat like it was the easiest thing in the world. Dropping it into his mouth, he smiled at her with only one side of his mouth. It was... well. Thea wasn't sure she was equipped to describe how she was feeling.

The day progressed from one filled with adrenaline to something more drowsy. She and Jonathan spent the rest of the day alone together, and they swapped stories of childhood. He took a beat here and there, wide-eyed and shocked at her story of survival. She had never spoken it out loud before, but she was proud of her resilience as he leaned forward in anticipation with each tale of how she narrowly escaped death. Most recently, with her elephant run-in.

"You are divine. Truly otherworldly. I want to hear everything, but I fear I've taken up so much of your day. Please forgive me, as I'm sure your family might want you home for the evening."

She looked up at the night sky not realizing how time slipped away from her. Mala would be so upset if she didn't make it back home soon. She didn't even recognize that her fate might have been in question by her family.

"Not to worry. Will you be here in this same area tomorrow?" Thea looked around the growing encampment. She wiped sand from her bum as she stood, nervous to see how Mala and the Boss felt about her recent abandonment of camp.

"I'll be anywhere you'd like me to be," John said earnestly.

Her chest swelled. "Goodnight, Jonathan."

"Goodnight, Thea."

He reached for her hand, and she allowed him to take it. He kissed the top of her knuckles and brushed a thumb over them, somehow locking in the kiss against her skin. Thea felt his deep brown eyes tracking her as she swung home.

CHAPTER 7

The following morning had been spent with Thea showing the crew around the outskirts of the jungle. Where they can forage for some edible plants, and what ones to avoid. John stayed close by her side. She felt protected. Before she went into her own tent, she reported her findings of other humans to Mala and the Boss. They had to trust her judgement, although they hated the encroaching on their territory.

"Are most of them safe?" Mala signed. Despite the line of questioning, Thea could tell her parents were glad she was alive and well.

"Yes. Well. Three out of the four I've met, at least. You can meet soon to get this all over with." Thea wasn't going to sign back this time because she was testing out how much they understood her. She climbed the nearest tree, flung herself off of the most optimal branch, freefalling only a moment before she caught the thick vine she was going for. Thea took her time swinging back out to the shore, mentally preparing to play host to the island's visitors. Currently, she was staring at the male her age. She ached to learn more about him in the limited time they would have together.

John's sleeves were rolled up to his elbows, showcasing his tanned, sweaty skin. Thea had the incredibly strong urge to lick him. She had seen other animals mating against her will, stumbling upon it from time to time, and then babies were born. Thea learned the basics from what her mom could tell her long ago and from what she observed in the wild.

"I like it, you know," she said, drawing his attention. "That you called me Wild One. If I had a middle name perhaps it would be Wild and my last name could be One." One. That's all she was, right? Singular. Alone but not entirely lonely. One.

"I'll call you whatever you want me to," he leaned into her, getting closer than she should allow. "As long as you keep letting us talk to you. I think I'd do anything to get to know you more." He started into her eyes, her soul really, and then leaned back, putting his hands behind his head. The wind picked up the top of his hair, caressing it. She thought to do the same just to see how it felt. It might be soft like the fuzz on the side of a tree, or maybe something more akin to gorilla fur, coarse and strong.

Just as Thea reached out to touch it, he peeked at her through one eye.

"Curious little thing, aren't you? I can feel you as you move." He sent another bright smile her way. Like he could be as still as she needed him to be so she could inspect. She doubted there would be bugs or small creatures in his hair like the other gorillas, but you just never know with strange humans showing up for the first time in her life. She swallowed hard with all of the saliva building up in her mouth. The ache she felt throughout her body was another adult reaction, she realized.

She ran her hand with care over the top of his head, sensing no bugs. Thea continued her pursuit of researching his body by picking at parts of his clothing, even peering down his shirt. He just laughed as she poked and prodded, crawling into his lap so she could go about her business as thoroughly as possible.

Jonathan never made a move to touch her in return. His strong hands were rooted deeply in the sand behind him, showcasing his strong chest in the process. He seemed as though he knew his way around the body of a woman. Unrushed. Sure.

Thea would do some research of her own, she bemused. She did not know how to write well, but she could sketch, just like her mother and father. She climbed off him, and he gave a pitying pout that made her chuckle. There was so little coal left, but she decided to spend the luxury on placing him on paper to have something for when they left. She produced her materials from the small linen sack she carried around her waist. It was heftier than usual, as it typically only contained a small canteen of water, a ration of food, and a small salve for her hands if they got too torn up.

John had been working all morning on setting up the base of the camp, so now when he stole a moment of rest underneath a palm tree on the sand, his face tilted to the sky carefree. His face cast transiently in shadow as the breeze caught and picked up nearby leaves. The scene was perfect.

She thought she was going unnoticed until his warm eyes slid toward her. A smile pulled at the corner of his mouth as they locked eyes.

"How should I pose for you, sweet Thea?"

"I think just like that is perfectly fine. I'm only capturing your face, so don't scrunch it up too much." She couldn't tell him she enjoyed the little lines that framed his eyes.

Jonathan cast his face back up to the sun, content to let her gaze upon him without shame or worry. She completed her sketch after several minutes, and allowed her feet to make noise to alert him that she was near. He opened his eyes in her direction as she handed him the drawing. She'd want it back, of course, but her subject deserved to see himself how she saw him. Incredibly handsome. Regal. Untouched by the wild. His pupils overtook the deep brown of his eyes.

"Come here." He spoke softly and gestured toward himself with two fingers. She complied, deciding not to fight his will this time. Thea was completely taken by him.

He brushed his thumb against her full bottom lip, pinking it up a bit. He moved his head up, his mouth breathing against hers a moment before he kissed her so gently, so sweetly, that her heart started to pick up speed just from the simplicity of it.

"Thank you for turning me into something unexpected. You... *you* are incredibly unexpected." He kept their eyes locked, this moment so monumental and so right. John leaned forward, keeping a hand on her knee as he continued. "As much as I don't want to say it, let's meet with the others to continue on about our day. I'm sure my mother won't be pleased that she's been left to her own devices for too long."

He got to his feet, wiping off the brush from the ground, and held out a hand to Thea.

"If we must," Thea huffed in fake discontent, and John smiled.

The group of four spent the rest of the afternoon rifling through the equipment and reserves of dry food.

Thea picked up this and that, inspecting each item, toddling between sneaking furtive glances at John and openly messing with equipment. When she snatched up a circular item with a handle and peered through it, everything got very large. It hurt her eyes and she didn't like it much. She handled nothing with care. Jonathan walked beside her attempting to grab everything she tossed into the air behind her.

Thea figured the sand was soft enough to catch these things. What was this flat board with legs that everything sat atop of? She overheard them mentioning a campsite. One of the shiphands came to help Mr. Ridgewell put up individual pointed tents. They seemed to struggle, which made her laugh.

"Do you need help?' Thea asked, trying to hide her snickering.

"No, we'll be quite alright. Just stay over there far away. Unless some of your monkey friends feel like giving us a hand with their opposable thumbs?" Chase huffed and looked behind her as though she could summon any animal at any time.

"Opposable thumbs?" Thea flexed her own and pointed every which way.

"Yes!" John said, after finally pitching successful housing for the evening. "It's what we have in common with some animals. Helps to grip things. Tigers don't have them but some primates do."

"Primates? Which ones are primates?" Thea had never been so curious. She needed to consume whatever they could offer her. Her own inquiring mind was never able to field the questions that kept her up at night.

"We'll get to everything, dear," Aggie filled in. "Would you like to stay for dinner?"

A traditional seated dinner was not something Thea would have ever expected after her mother died. She walked nervously around the food being heated over the small fire made on the beach. These people were strangers, and she needed to get back to her own family. They were probably worried about her, but too afraid to approach the growing campsite.

"I think I'll have to go soon, but thank you for asking. I'll get my own dinner." She spoke only to John then. She quickly pivoted to turn away, and a gentle touch on her shoulder stopped her in her tracks.

"Please, stay." John brushed a hand against her shoulder. "Now that I have my tent up, I have plenty of room to host you if you're interested in more little luxuries. I completely understand if not. But you would have your own cot." He stiffened, momentarily concerned that he crossed a boundary. For having such a commanding presence, she hadn't felt like he was controlling her next move.

She turned and looked for guidance in his soft expression. It was hard to breathe when his attention was so rapt upon her. He flitted easily between fun and protective in the short time she had known him.

"Sure. I'll stay with you." She was certain she'd never be able to say no to spending more time with him.

Thea had officially spent the entire day with the island's intruders. As the sun set, she walked where the water met sand, hoping to calm her mind, telling Jonathan that she needed a moment alone. She might be able to use this group to get information on her family. She barely remembered something about a grandmother and father on her father's side, but her own mother didn't speak kindly about her own parents. Anything might be better than something though.

Once again, Jonathan brought her out of reverie, approaching her once the sun had set.

"Ready to go inside?" He gestured toward the tent, and she went willingly with her hand in his.

CHAPTER 8

For the first time in her life, Thea had a truly luxurious sleeping arrangement. The sheets were fluffy, and so was the pillow. She found so much joy in fluffing around the blanket, giggling every time she did so. Entertaining herself was an easy feat. She'd been doing it her whole life.

"I can see you're making yourself comfortable. Good." Jonathan came to stand beside her where she lay in her cot. His was on the other side of the tent. It was much larger overall than the structures she was used to. This one could house a makeshift kitchen, a small table in between the two cots, and his personal luggage.

"I really am. I can't wait to tell my family about this adventure in the morning." She laughed and fluttered her feet some more. She was likely dirty for their standards, but if he didn't mind neither did she.

"We can make some breakfast, and then perhaps..." John shook his head, stopping himself.

Thea sat up straight in her cot.

"Perhaps what?"

"Well I feel as though perhaps I'm just now earning your trust. I don't want to ruin it by asking to meet your family—the animals. But hopefully sometime soon? We don't have much time here." He rubbed the back of his neck. John had a job to do, and she might be able to help him.

"Maybe I'll let you meet one of them at a time. Just one. And then she can determine if you can meet the others." Thea pulled the blanket up to her chin, feeling exposed under his gaze.

"We will do whatever you are comfortable with. I only fear that if we don't get to them before Ridgewell, things might not go as smoothly as we intended. That heathen is truly something else," John finished, rubbing his hands up and down his face before refocusing on her.

"I'll be the one to make sure that everything goes well. If you need it for your job, I don't want to stop you. I can help show you what plants do what and what smaller fish are good to eat and cook. My mother told me that she had formal schooling and taught me to read and write a little, but I know a lot about the island," Thea said, nodding her head.

"I'm sure that you do. Which is why any help at all would be incredible." He pulled off his outer shirt, revealing muscular arms in a tank top, as he was already wearing shorts before she walked into the tent.

"I'll be right here if you need anything at all." He gestured to a glass of water on the table. "That one is for you in case you get thirsty in the middle of the night."

How very convenient. She felt parched already. She hadn't thought about housing water like this for herself near her makeshift bed. He captured her hand between both of his, turning it over and kissing the back of it. "Dream sweet, Wild One. There's much to do in the morning." He dropped her hand all too quickly in Thea's opinion. He walked to his cot, turned out the lantern, and darkness fell in the tent.

Thea drifted off easily, albeit stunned by the contact his lips made on her skin again. However, three hours into her slumber, she awoke when lightning struck. The crack reminded her of the gunshot from the day prior and her heart started beating out of her chest once again. After a moment of reorientation, she realized it was a tropical storm brewing past the coast.

She sat upright, sweating. The air was stagnant in the tent, and yet another bolt of lightning crashed through the sky somewhere, illuminating the tent just a fraction. At that moment, she saw John turned onto his stomach. He must have been sleeping fitfully as well. A glistening line of sweat trailed down the center of his back. His muscles twitched, and his head bore deeper into the pillow. Was he awake like she was?

"John," she whispered gently into the dark tent.

He stirred for a moment, rustling the sheets in his wake until he settled again. He must be having a nightmare. Those, she was used to. Thea felt the strangest inkling to go to him and comfort him. Just when she built up the courage to kick a leg out from under the blanket, a series of lightning strikes illuminated the tent. He was turned onto his back now, the front of him completely on display. His brows were furrowed, like he was worried or frustrated. With the last bit of light, she caught the tenting of his manhood beneath his blanket. Her heart picked up in her chest. She needed to go to him, fix what ailed him.

"John," she tried again. "Are you awake?"

"Trying not to be," John responded softly.

"Were you having a dream?"

"Yes, I was. It was nothing. Go back to sleep, Wild One."

"You keep calling me that."

"I'm not inclined to stop."

Thea could hear his smile when he said it. She yearned to put her own lips on his. Make it all better. Helping one another sleep was altruistic. Thea would be doing him a favor. She wanted to learn all about what made him tick and everything in between.

"Can I come over? I don't like being this close to the lightning. I'm usually much further inland when I sleep. It's unnerving." Thea knew she was testing her luck, but some otherworldly force drove them together without explanation.

"I'm not sure that's a good idea right now," John said in the darkness, tension brimming behind his words. The feeling of rejection didn't stop Thea. There was something else lined in his words.

Thea rose anyway, took a few careful steps toward him, and lifted the covers for herself.

"Even the animals huddle together. They say it's for safety."

His body tightened and shimmied as far away from her as he could. He didn't make it far because he was so large, and the bed was truly too small for the both of them. She knew why he turned away, and it wasn't because she was being rejected. She witnessed the evidence minutes ago.

"Are you frightened of me?" She said plainly. "I won't hurt you"

He chuckled softly. "No. I'm not afraid of you. I'm afraid of what I might turn into around you."

"And what might that be? I can speak to all sorts of animals," she teased. Maybe one day he would learn the extent of that truth.

"I'm worried that I might..." He turned fully away from her now. But he didn't kick her out of his cot.

She inched closer, wrapping an arm around him. She nuzzled into his neck from behind, inhaling deeply. Her own fingers did plenty of exploring, but she yearned to have someone else conjure the release she gave herself often.

"Worried that you might what?"

At that, he turned around toward her, moving his hand on her upper thigh. Thunder struck.

BOOM.

His brow remained creased, eyes fixated on her lips.

CRACK.

The storm that raged outside couldn't compare to the war brewing between two people who had just met. They hadn't known each other. But it didn't matter.

His body flexed toward her, and he brushed her sweat-soaked hair away from her face. Both of his hands encircled the back of her neck. She couldn't move. Didn't want to.

"Can I?" Jonathan's eyes moved down to her lips, and his hard chest started to heave deeply. Despite naivety in this arena, she knew what he was asking.

"Yes, please," Thea responded, pushing her hands into his hair.

Jonathan's lips met hers in the most sensual way. She tingled all the way down to her toes and felt pleasantly light-headed. This was Thea's second-ever kiss. The first John gave her was one of acknowledgement and appreciation for her gift.

She had minimal advice to recall what to do in this situation, so she did what her body sought fit. Her hands intertwined around the back of his head, drawing him closer. He smelled a little of sweat, and her inner primate beat its chest, wanting to claim him any way she could. His tongue parted her mouth, and she let him in, as desperate as the summer months yearning for water to wash away humid air.

Her strong, long legs used leverage to get on top to straddle him. His hardness felt so delicious in between her slit. Thea paused for a moment to feel around his chest, exploring the feeling of another human being before he crashed her mouth against his own once again. He was fervent, possessive, and breathing heavy.

"We shouldn't be doing this. I—I don't want to take advantage of you." John pulled back, cradling the back of her neck. He sounded pained.

"If anything, I'm taking advantage of you." She ground herself against his hard cock, only knowing that this felt good and right and needed. Her core started to draw up tighter and tighter, waiting to snap.

"Oh, fuck, Thea, I'm going to come if you keep doing that." John reared back up, biting her lip. She invited a little pain. It's all she knew. The softness he evoked in her was something she'd have to explore later.

"That's what I do with my fingers, see?' Thea reached between them, playing with her sensitive bud while stroking herself against him. She was going to feel that perfect liquid in between her legs. She wondered what his release looked like.

"Oh god, Thea. You touch yourself? So you know?" He sounded relieved this time.

"I know how to make myself feel good, and I know about human anatomy." Thea left it at that.

Her legs tightened on either side of his hips, and he thrust underneath her, dry-fucking her through his underwear. She could feel wetness from the both of them, and that only made her hotter and stickier than she had any right to be in this crowded tent. She ground against him harder and faster, reveling in every second.

"Jonath—" she started to scream, and he clamped a large hand around her mouth. Thea's sex clamped around nothing, clenching and releasing against John's hardness. The ecstasy

Zia Tyree

was completely different when she did it with someone else. Much better. She wanted more.

"Your release is not for others to hear. Only me. Only ever me," he pleaded with her. It must be unladylike to allow others to hear what they were doing to each other.

Just as she was coming down from the high of being handled so possessively, John flipped her onto her back and pushed aside her underthings.

She could barely make out what he was doing until he whispered, "Suck, Thea."

Thea opened her mouth to receive two of John's thick fingers, shocked at herself for finding someone perhaps more wild than she. She sucked more fervently, hoping to please John readily. He pulled them out of her mouth with a *pop*, and trailed them all the way down in between her legs.

"Open for me, I need to do this just once. I need to feel your heat clamp around some part of me because I know it's too early and too wrong to fuck you like this," John said, part command, part desperation.

Thea parted her legs for him, wetness dripping down onto the sheets below. The two fingers that were in her wanting mouth just moments ago parted her sex and got to work. Thick, perfect digits entered her swiftly, pulling all the way out to her peaking bud, and all the way back inside her again. She bucked against his fingers like they were her own, this sensation more familiar. But his fingers were more pleasurable because they were so much larger than her own. She hadn't completely come down from her first orgasm, so the second one wasn't hard for John to chase down.

She was swollen and ready as the second massive wave hit her. John claimed her mouth again, this time with an aggression she searched for under the surface and everything hit her with perfect synchrony.

It was torture.

It was madness.

It was perfect.

CHAPTER 9

Thea didn't know when they fell asleep. She only remembered being distinctly disappointed that she nodded off before getting the chance to return the favors he repeatedly bestowed upon her.

She played with Jonathan's hair, stirring him awake.

"Good morning, Wild One." He smiled sleepily at her.

"Good morning, Jonathan." Thea reached her hand down to his already-erect member.

"Nah-ah. None of that. We have a big day ahead of us," he lightly chastised.

"Why not? I want to learn. I want to learn everything with you." Thea smiled in return.

"Because what I feel for you is not transactional. Making you happy last night made me happy, and that's all I need." John sighed softly, pulling her hand to his chest, and kissing her palm before covering it with his own. He shut his eyes once more as he said, "We'll start with breakfast, attempt to not be too cheeky around my mother, and if I'm lucky, I get to meet a member of your family. How does that sound?"

"And then... do I come back here? Or do you continue your research alone?"

"I'd prefer to not do anything alone while I'm on this island." He moved to be on top of her, enough for her to notice his hardness against her. The message was clear. He needed her to know what she did to him, but he wouldn't go near her like that. Not yet. He licked his way up the side of her neck, and nibbled on her ear for a moment before hopping off the cot.

"I need to wash. May I go to my stream, and come back here after? I'd like to discuss the meeting with my family before I bring you to them." She turned onto her side, watching him pull up his trousers.

"I do not wish to keep you any longer than you want to be kept. You're too wild for me to tame fully," he said, bringing her forehead to his lips and kissing it gently. Thea reluctantly hopped out of the cot, finding the other half of her underthings.

"And if I want to be tamed?" Thea tossed back on her way out. Something that looked like hope passed through his expression.

She wouldn't be able to stay away from him long if she tried. He gave her an easy, certain smile in return, shrugging his shoulders at her implication. One smile felt like a drop in the ocean of what she wanted from him.

Thea climbed the nearest trunk and flew off, snatching the closest vine to her, connecting looking ahead at the canopy before her. She enjoyed the thick smell of hot earth far beneath her. Soft enough to catch her if she fell, but she never would. She danced among the greenery, always finding her own rhythm and peace.

She approached her favorite stream. It supported supple leaves that, when picked apart and mashed lightly, created a cleansing paste. She enjoyed smelling like the trees she lived around. It was a small piece of her self esteem that created proof she deserved to live here. The more she became adapted to her environment, the easier the assimilation was. Beyond this, Thea hoped that it would mask the scent of her sex for fear of her family's heightened sense of smell. She was cavorting with humans, of all things, and Thea anticipated her family would be upset. But the vitriol she experienced once finding them at their familiar homestead shocked her beyond measure.

Mala and the Boss were side by side, as per usual, leading on open forum discussion about the humans.

"Hiya, everyone!" Thea greeted. "I've spoken with the humans. Most are good. One is... less than good."

THEA. Where have you been? Mala stood up, chuffing and gesturing Thea to move toward them and in the front of the crowd. Thea was hoping for a more one-on-one confrontation, but this was her best chance at getting the truth.

"You did it again! You spoke to me. In English. In my head." Thea was convinced she heard something and wasn't going to back down for anything in the world. Out of habit, she signed along everything she said to ensure her message was clear for all of the creatures congregating in one spot.

We always knew it would come to this. Oh, Boss. What do we tell our sweet girl?

Thea glanced around, feeling trapped among the animals for the first time in her life.

She deserves the truth, at this point. A new voice she couldn't pinpoint.

Boss, I think it's time! Another. Her own mind was cacophonous.

The voices grew.

It's our turn to talk to—

We can help, Th—

I don't know how I feel about visitors, but we could—

Everyone, calm down!

The thick air was suffocating her from within. Her senses were heightened. So many voices. She squatted down, putting her hands around her ears, as if it would stifle the noise of the forest.

How about we start by making you feel a bit less... crazy? The Boss finally silenced the rest.

The next hour spent in the presence of the group nearly split her head in two. The voices weren't just of the gorillas. No. Full English. In her head. It was explained to her that she was chosen. Chosen by the elders to expose their secret. They were able to put their thoughts into the minds of others. This gift extended to the animals that they chose around them, as well. They planned to reveal all this to her human mother, but Mala was only able to let her know the day before she passed. Thea may never know the extent of the conversation that they had, mother-to-mother.

Mala and the Boss refused to relay what their actual names were, but only because they preferred Thea to call them what she always did. Another new name might make her head explode, anyway.

It would be like if you called your mom by her first name, Emilia, and your father, Nathaniel, Mala said.

"Emilia," she whispered. The name rocked her deeply. It felt like a lullaby. Her mother's name felt deep under her skin, an unwatered seed just below her feet.

"Nathaniel," she said a little louder. Now this name was foreign. It wasn't any more or less wrong than Emilia, just new. Nathaniel felt trapped, underneath a sheet of ice she'd never be able to smash through. Hot tears dripped down Thea's face, one at a time.

"Do you know their last names? Perhaps I can ask the humans. They seem nice enough! Maybe they can help me find more family."

Mala bristled at this.

If that is what you wish. Her voice was more somber than Thea anticipated.

"Well. Maybe. This is all very..." Thea gestured around herself and to the gathered animals. Her breath came quickly, threatening to pull her under.

Now, now. If you wish to decipher your lineage we will support you. Your mother, she just... she doesn't wish to see you leave forever. Would you come back? The Boss said.

Thea's breath stilled as his large hand rubbed the side of her arm. She was surprised at the open affection the Boss displayed in front of the pack.

This was their fear. Their true fear. That she would leave them, never to return. How could she? This was her chosen family. They saved her, fed her, clothed her when she was alone. She'd never truly leave. But she might have to temporarily in order to solve the mystery that was her life.

"I would never leave you, not from here." She put her pointer finger right against the Boss's heart. He ducked his head to avoid showing emotion. "It's my duty to fulfill my parent's dream. Or at least to figure out what it was. Maybe seek my own company? If I were to do this temporarily, would you still support me?"

Mala and the Boss looked at each other, stood tall, and beat their chest. Soon, the entire forest was awake. Alive. Shaking under her feet with the promise of understanding a new path forward.

We stand with you!

We love you!

We honor you.

Thea threw out her hands and spun around in the same way she did when she was very little, catching the rays of light through the trees in her palms, savoring the heat.

Chapter 10

Thea flipped open the flap of the tent she shared with Jonathan overnight, just to find him gone. What she found instead were both of their cots, pushed together, the sheets covering the tops, pillows fluffed. Her heart warmed. She wasn't sure what this was the start of, but she knew it held the promise of answers. Regardless, she felt full for the first time in years. The first time she went to the river on her own was refreshing. Her first successful swing between the vines was invigorating. But this was something different entirely.

She imagined what a very large bed could look like. The two cots seemed to work just fine, but the things the Queen must have must be incredibly lavish in comparison.

She inched closer to the nightstand and saw a few books stacked on top of each other. The words were bigger than she could read, although she could make out a few. Salt air clung to the cloth, mixing with the salt of their sweat from the night before.

Just as she was about to poke around further, she heard the tent flap. With a smile on her face, she whipped around expecting to meet her lover, or whoever he was, and instead she faced the cruel Mr. Ridgewell.

"Hello, Mr. Ridgewell," she said stiffly. "I wasn't expecting you here." She stood taller, crossing her arms over her bandaged chest.

"Hello Miss... whatever your last name is." He waved a hand dismissively. "Are you here to take us to the gorillas?"

"No. At least, not until this afternoon. That's what they agreed to." She looked around briefly for any potential weapon she could use in case he advanced.

"That's quite alright. I suppose. I'm looking for John. Have you seen him?"

He was searching, but not for John. She knew this for certain.

"No, I haven't. I was looking for him as well. Did he take a trip back to your main vessel?"

And as if the gods answered, the tent flap reopened.

"Chase," Aggie stated plainly. For being so petite, her aura packed quite the punch. Her mood quickly turned when she pushed him aside to take a peek at her. "Ah, Miss Thea. So glad to see you this morning. Are you going to join us for another day at the beach? I have more equipment for you to discover."

"Yes! I would like that very much. And this afternoon, I would like to take you and your son to meet my family. Would this help you in your research?"

Aggie smiled wide. "Are you sure it's not too soon? Do you think they would be open to us? We would simply start with a greeting, draw some basic sketches, and go from there."

"What we need to do is study their brutish behavior in this godforsaken jungle," Mr. Ridgewell sneered.

"No. You will not be joining us, Chase." Aggie let the indignancy and bite of using his first name hang on her tongue like something sour.

"It's Mr. Ridgewell. And I will be going."

"It's Chase, and no you certainly will not. Stay behind and tend to our things," Aggie said, hooking her arm around the young woman. "You've made enough of an impression on this sweet girl."

He rolled his eyes and muttered, "She started it."

"What was that?" Aggie snapped.

"Nothing, Dr. Perch. Nothing at all." Mr. Ridgewell strode out of the tent, and the tightness in Thea's chest loosened with his absence.

"How about we look for my son? He has some things he'd like to show you." Aggie

Zia Tyree

wiggled her eyebrows in amusement, but Thea couldn't discern its meaning. She smiled alongside her savior, and strode out once again into the midday sun.

————————

"No, John! I just can't do it!"

"It's been one afternoon! You certainly can."

Thea began to shake the textbook violently, as if she could shake the words off of the pages. She thought it was silly this was called a textbook because all books had text. And pictures. Thea enjoyed the pictures much more than the text. There were pictures of birds she didn't recognize above text she couldn't read. She ripped one picture of a finch right out because she liked it and wanted to keep it in her room. John's mouth went slack until he laughed a big belly laugh.

She held it out. "For my room. This would be nice."

He laughed harder.

"What is so funny? I wanted it." She flipped over the picture, happy to see there was another bird that piqued her interest.

"You're quite endearing. I can cut some out for you, if you'd like. With scissors. So the edges aren't jagged?" He ran one hand along her back and held the picture with her. The gentle caress was only a reminder of what she had been missing.

Thea often took what she wanted without remorse because she did not have much to begin with. The book wouldn't miss the page, but she would miss the finch.

Earlier, after pushing what she learned was called a microscope off of a table, John attempted to show her what he thought was going to be a less destructive activity.

Reading.

"Let's sound out some more words together."

"This is quite frustrating. I don't know that I can bear anymore for today." Thea crossed her arms with mild petulance. She wanted to be worldly and sophisticated, not... untamed.

"How about we strike a small bargain?" John said teasingly.

He rounded on her, rubbing both hands up and down her shoulders. "For every word you get right, you'll get a reward."

"What kind of a reward? I'm not sure there's anything else you can give me that I don't already have." Thea lied straight through her teeth. Hygiene products. A proper bath with proper soap. Meals she didn't have to procure for herself. Come to think of it, there were plenty of rewards she wouldn't mind having.

"I'm not thinking about anything tangible. Although, I'd like to find a way to give you anything you wanted."

A chill ran down Thea's spine despite the warmth surrounding them.

He moved his large hand to her lower back, guiding her to sit at the table. Her normally tense shoulders melted, as he put his hands on either side of her, leaning over her and the book. John's hot breath whispered in her ear, "Read."

Thea placed both palms in her lap, hoping to center herself.

"The." She underlined the word with her forefinger. Thea turned to look at him, straightening her back.

"Well that's not fair. That's your name without the 'a' at the end. I need you to try a little harder."

She rolled her eyes and went back to the text book.

"The s-sm-small ro-rob-robin..." she looked up for reassurance. "Is that right? This bird" —she tapped rapidly— "this one is called a robin? I don't see any of those here."

"Correct. Your intonation of 'in' at the end there should be 'in' not 'een'. Like, the word 'inside'."

Thea moved to stand up and demand her prize. He gently pushed her back down.

"Keep going." He urged her on, fighting a smile.

"I thought I got a reward. I'd like to see it." She looked back up at him. His hands started to massage her shoulders.

Ohhh... that was nice.

Fine. She'd continue.

"Robins eat a v-vari-variety of food." She paused. He nodded. "Ins-inse-insects. P-pla-plants. Fr-fro-frit?" She couldn't make out the last word.

"Fruit. It looks funny on the page, but the 'u' and 'i' together can make an 'oo' sound."

Jonathan worked his hands into her neck. She moaned. He paused for a beat.

"Once you understand the titles, you can pick out a book you have interest in, and we can read it together. And when I'm gone, you can keep as many as you'd like. To remember me by," he said, his perfect smile faltering briefly.

"What if I went with you?" She spat the question out before thinking, as she often did.

"Went with us?" Jonathan's tone refused to betray his meaning. His hands worked her shoulders for a moment longer.

"I have questions." She rubbed the corner of the worn page between her thumb and forefinger, pretending to be interested in it. His hands worked their way up to her neck, kneading out years worth of tension from climbing trees and whipping through vines.

"Questions about what? I'd love to help in any way I can," John turned her chair around with Thea still in it. He used his thumb to stroke her inner thighs, not with suggestion but with comfort. Her pulse quickened nonetheless.

"I learned—*remembered* the first names of my parents. I'm hoping you can help me find more of my human family. Or really, anything else about my past. I have nothing." She turned her hands to the sky, looking at her empty palms.

Thea gave up on pretense, letting the tears fill up her eyes. Jonathan backed off on the suggestive touching immediately in favor of a hug. She pushed her face into his chest, worried at how he'd perceive her crying twice in one day.

"I'll do anything you ask, and more, if you'll let me." The second time he spoke into her ear, it was a declaration without performance.

She could only nod as she pulled back from his strong warm chest, staring at his full lips. She perked her head up for a chaste kiss, and he returned it with the ease of knowing someone for a lifetime.

"What book would you like to tear into next, Wild One?"

Chapter 11

A tropical breeze flowed through Thea's hair, and she knew she could no longer avoid the meeting.

"The Perch family. I would like to introduce you to Mala and the Boss."

Aggie and Jonathan approached simultaneously, closing their fists, bending down at the waist, preparing to walk on all fours.

"What is it that you're doing?" Thea smiled a bit.

"Umm, actually. I'm not entirely sure. Do they need our scent to know that we're not a threat?" Jonathan said, straightening up, sounding a bit embarrassed at his lack of knowledge around the gorillas.

Haha. They're no threat to me. The Boss stood a little straighter and crossed his arms.

Play nice. Thea said back in her head, testing out the communication. It proved to go both ways, and she was just now realizing it. She only hoped they couldn't read her thoughts all of the time. Her cheeks flushed with the implication. The Boss staggered back a bit. Never had she been able to interject her own thoughts onto another.

Aggie looked at Thea and then back to The Boss. "Did he... Did he say something to you?"

Jonathan looked on in wonder. Thea realized that her brow was scrunched, and she was gesturing.

"Yes." Thea said easily. No point in lying.

"So, what exactly are you communicating to him? He looks quite protective," John smiled in wonder at the much larger creature before him. Thea thought he might have been intimidated by The Boss, but he was more interested in getting to know him more than anything.

"I told him to play nice." She looked pointedly at The Boss again before acknowledging Mala. "And this is my mom."

Oh, I appreciate you saying that. Mala reached out a large palm to tap Jonathan on the shoulder. While he was appreciative of The Boss, Jonathan shrunk against the physical contact.

I'm the one he should be afraid of. Very afraid. Mala leaned into Jonathan and sniffed pointedly. Then huffed. Jonathan gave a nervous smile, feeling the threat whether he understood completely or not. Aggie stepped in then. She did a little bow, trying to level mother-to-mother.

"I think you raised a truly splendid girl," Aggie said with discipline and respect. She then backed away to give Mala some much-needed space.

Hmm. I've decided that I like her. Because she is correct. The young man, on the other hand, will have to win me over. I can smell you on him. Would you like to explain yourself?

"No, I don't want to explain myself," Thea huffed back.

I wasn't going to say anything judgemental. You're of fertile age. You are allowed to bear offspring if you wish. I'm just not sure about the logistics. The Boss chuffed at his mate, seeming to laugh even with the massive weight of his arms.

Mala raised her hands in frustration, clapping the sides of her face.

BOSS! This is not funny. We are two girls having a girl's talk!

"I'm so sorry, Wild One, care to elaborate what's happening?" John leaned over to Thea, tilting his head at the massive primates.

"I keep forgetting to translate. I'm not sure I want to translate these exact words around Dr. Perch." Thea rubbed the back of her neck.

"No need to fret, dear. We're just here to see them in their natural habitat. We don't even need to ask questions." The most shocking part of it all was how easily Thea was believed. The Perches must have sensed something much larger was at play.

"No, it's okay. I want you to have what you need. Mom, Dad. This family would like to follow you, track your movements, what you eat, and the like. Does that sound alright?"

Thea could have sworn that The Boss blushed at her calling him exactly what he was. Her dad. He raised her, and that was the easiest way to describe him to brand new people.

We are agreeable. Is this for the same science your mother performed?

"It seems so. They would like to gain more knowledge for conservation efforts in their own home." She turned toward the Perches. "They are open to your research. She wants to know if it's the same type of research my mother performed?" Thea looked expectantly.

"Who was your mother, dear?" Dr. Perch.

Thea spent the next several hours sharing stories from Mala's perspective, and the Perch family studied them fiercely.

John found a boulder to perch upon with pen and pencil in hand, he drew the flora and fauna around him. He stole glances at Thea every chance he got from under thick lashes. She was certain he knew she caught him from time to time. And that alone made her shiver.

You know, this is how your mother described your father. Very intentional. An artist. Furrowed brow. I think she might approve. Mala said into her mind with mild resignation.

Approve of what? Thea feigned innocence.

Oh, you know what. The way you look at him. I don't care that you just met. There's something between you. I can smell the hormones. Mala rolled her eyes at that last bit. Mala was always one to have a strong personality, but Thea was shocked to see a true-to-form eye roll come from the massive gorilla.

Thea snuggled into her side, watching the Perches work their own sort of magic.

It's nice to have a conversation with you. I knew you understood, but I didn't know the depth.

I would understand you with or without the ability to speak into your mind, Dear One. Humans are very simple.

Mala and Thea shared a mutual chuckle as they looked at each other.

Thea supposed she was right. She wanted John more than she'd wanted most things. Even finding out about her own heritage.

Chapter 12

"I have something to show you, Thea," John said at the end of the day. He had already exposed her to so much, her brain was overstimulated with what else it could possibly be.

"I'm not so sure that I can handle much more. Today was a lot to say the least." Thea wrung her hands together. She didn't enjoy uncertain things. So much had already gotten in the way of routine.

"It won't take long. Then I can bring you back to your home. What do you say?" John reached out his strong hand, with long fingers and Thea couldn't help herself but lay her palm in his again just to be near his warmth.

"I'll give you one more hour. And that will be it for today. Tomorrow you can have more time, I'm sure you'll need it with the time constraint."

"It would be an honor to spend even an hour more with you if you permitted it." John's eyes glistened in the falling sun, reflecting back the earth around them. His pull was irresistible.

She said a temporary goodbye to her parents, and John shook The Boss's massive hand—a gesture he taught them quickly as the sign of good will and greetings.

Dr. Perch walked a distance ahead of them, giving them the space they needed to converse freely. Her small head was hunched forward, still furiously scribbling away, despite running into several low-hanging branches.

"Mother, I'm going to show Thea some of the new equipment delivered today. We'll catch back up later," John said, looking at Thea with heat in his eyes.

"Right, right, very well." Dr. Perch spared no more than a glance, waving goodbye in their direction.

Thea's palms started to sweat, not with exertion, but with anticipation. Would he kiss her again? She hoped soon. She hoped for many things with this strange man who wasn't so strange at all. He was foreign, but his body was not. He looked so proper, but underneath it all they were simply the same. The primal need to climb him like one of her trees ran deep, but what was the point if they were going to be separated soon?

Dr. Perch went out of view, and they were truly alone once again.

She was lifted off of her feet and carried toward a tree off the path. Jonathan pressed her back into the warm bark, and she loved the way her skin felt raw against it.

"I couldn't wait a second longer," he panted into her ear, and wrapped his hand around her hair pulling her neck to the side. He licked from between her breasts, up her neck, and to her ear. She shuddered.

How could he enjoy the taste of her sweat? She found it a rare opportunity that he would want her scent on his body like she wanted his. It was an entirely primal thing to trade sweat and immerse yourself into this kind of contact. Thea kissed him back with all she had, still feeling novice in the process. John didn't seem to mind the effort on her end. Her core was lined up against him, feeling him grow harder with each pass of her tongue against his. She needed to feel release. And soon. He pulled back, shaking his hair off of his sweated brow.

"The way I need to feel you is nearly too consuming. I've never felt so..." He trailed off. "Wait—your back!" He moved her off of the tree, and planted her gently on her feet. Suddenly aware of the position he had put her in. "I'm so sorry! Are you okay?" He turned her around to inspect her skin, running hand along the light scratches on her lower back.

"I'm quite alright! I loved that. Let's keep walking back to camp." Thea blushed and pushed her long dark hair out of her face with both hands in a sordid attempt to refresh herself after the growing tension between her legs consumed   her   thoughts. Once she saw the opening of his tent, her heart started to race. It usually only picked up speed with the physical exertion of swinging vine to vine. When she felt the most free. She felt free to be herself with John, too.

He held the flap open further, gesturing her inside. "After you, love."

There was a large contraption set up on the side of the tent, pointing at a large piece of what appeared to be canvas.

She walked up to it, sniffed the metal. It smelled like the ship's exhaust and oil. It was nearly indistinguishable from the other forms of tools and equipment, beside the fact that it looked golden instead of silver, and there was a strip of something coming out of it. She reached out to pull on it, when John gently put her hand back down by her side.

"Why can't I touch it? That's how I learn. Touching things," Thea said haughtily.

He laughed and cracked another gleaming smile. "I'm aware. But this is going to turn on, and if you pull at that, I won't be able to show you what I want to."

With that, he gently took her shoulders, and positioned her to the side of the machine, directing her attention to the blank canvas hanging.

"I'm just not sure what the point of staring at canvas is. This is not productive."

"Just wait a moment while I get it started, Wild One. Always so impatient." He just shook his head. The gesture held no malice, only entertainment.

Just when she was going to go against his wishes and inspect the equipment, it roared to life at his hands.

It was a picture. But it was... moving? Her eyes grew wide, and she turned on a heel to him.

"This is terrifying! What is this? What are these small people doing moving?"

"Thea, dear, they can't hurt you! They're not real! Just images in motion. Now watch."

Thea moved closer, ready to touch them. She only created a larger shadow so she pulled back. There was a group of people walking around outside of a large building. Two of them were walking hand in hand. The lighting of realization hit her square in the chest.

"John! John. I'm—" She started to back up slowly.

"I know it's very overwhelming, but this is outside of where we work. This is from some time ago, but it was the only footage I was allowed to bring outside of the facility. I thought you might enjoy seeing—" She put a hand on his chest.

"Go back! I need to go back. Please go back to that couple. The one right there! Holding hands!"

"I like watching them as well. They were researchers like my mother and I are..." he trailed off for a moment with the realization. The dark hair, the bone structure of the woman. These were her parents.

Thea reached out a hand, yearning to be closer to the faces who looked so much like hers. She recognized her mother from her back at first. The back she would climb daily, to be carried around like the gorillas. The same long, dark hair. The tall man looking down adoringly at her mother had to have been her father. It was blurry, but she knew beyond a shadow of a doubt that this was the man who loved her mother with every breath he had. Her own long arms mirrored his.

"Oh my. Wild One. Are these your biological parents? They were top researchers for the Queen. They went missing, heading for a different island around..."

"Twenty-two years ago?" Thea felt a hot tear trickle down her cheek. She couldn't look at John. She couldn't look away from the image before her. John continued to play it. The couple trotted up the steps of the building. Her father opened the door for her, and her mother rubbed her hand on his shoulder in thanks. Nathaniel followed quickly behind her, clearly not wanting to miss out on being near her.

"I have to know. I need to know about them. Their lives. What were they like? Who would know? Your mother?"

"So wait—that means they never reached their true destination. This island is the first in a chain of islands. The Crown was looking everywhere but here." John was pacing. "The only person around them during the peak of their research was actually Mr. Ridgewell. He was an explorer like them. They frequently went on missions together, but he let them come to what must have been this island alone." The picture shuddered to a stop. "You look so much like your mother. I'm surprised he hasn't made the connection yet."

"Let's ask your mother to review this. She might have some more information." Thea nibbled on her lip with nervous anticipation.

Zia Tyree

CHAPTER 13

Dr. Perch was summoned and watched the film intently. Over and over.

"I've seen this before. They use it during orientation for new scientists at the University as an homage to those who have come before them. It represents the joy of those coming into work for the Queen daily. Some notice the couple, some don't. It's so clear to me now." She turned toward Thea. "Those are your parents? Nathaniel and Emilia Underwood."

"Underwood." Every time she tried a new name or word out on her tongue it felt foreign, but not this time. It felt waking up from a dream and finally remembering the ending. It was her last name.

"If Chase was on their team, wouldn't he have known this island was near their destination? Would he have not sought them out along the chain of islands?"

"Maybe not. The Crown might not have been able to fund another trip for fear of him not coming back as well. But their disappearance was so strange. They were expert navigators. And we had little to no trouble getting here." Dr. Perch started tapping her foot and an index finger against her lips in motion together.

"Something about this isn't adding up, Mother. Do you think the navigation records of their projected course were accurate? What about the crew log?"

"Well, I think the only way we'd be able to confirm any of this would be to pull the archives back at the university. I doubt anyone else would reopen the investigation considering the Queen's involvement in closing the case. Just an incredibly unfortunate accident."

But Aggie didn't sound convinced at her own conclusion. The glances Dr. Perch and her son were exchanging turned Thea's core sour. The last time her stomach was this turned around was when she attempted to do a double back flip off of a vine. Not a good idea.

"Let's ask Mr. Ridgewell directly. I need answers." Thea nearly stormed off before Aggie caught her wrist.

"Child, no. Not yet. Let us figure out a plan. If Ridgewell knows more than he's leading on, then we need to figure out who else may be involved. There could be many limbs to this, and cutting off a pinky finger might not do too much damage." Aggie stood now with her back straight and her hands on her hips.

"Goodness, mother. Never thought I'd hear you talk about chopping off body parts."

"Just because I haven't said it out loud doesn't mean I'm not thinking about it! Matter of fact—there's one particular body part I wouldn't mind cutting off—"

"Mother!" Jonathan said stopping her before she could go any further.

The quip eased the tension in the room, but only slightly. The air was thick with anticipation of starting yet another project. Thea's mind was stretching beyond belief.

"How do we do our own research without tipping him off? Everyone here is on his payroll except for us," Thea said as she ran rough hands through her long hair.

"We need to send a message from the ship back home. If someone can go into the archives and send word back to see if there was any alteration in the itinerary, then we know for certain that Chase isn't here for the right reasons." Aggie reassured Thea, calming down from her previous statement.

"Don't worry, Thea. We'll try to keep you away from him as much as possible and get to the bottom of this." Jonathan rubbed his hand against her lower back as she stared at the film starting from the top again. She took a deep breath, steeling her resolve.

"We have to put him near my family. I need to see how he interacts with them to understand his intentions. They can smell a liar a mile away."

"Literally?" John was capable of believing anything at this point.

"Well. Sort of. It's pretty close with them, actually." Thea gave a small smile.

CHAPTER 14

"Are you absolutely sure this is a good idea?"

"Not entirely. I wouldn't say espionage is my strong suit, but I am the only one who knows Morse code. And who can row this boat by themselves..." Jonathan shrugged. "Well. That's beyond the point. If you stay in my tent, there are weapons you can defend yourself with should Ridgewell get close to you. Do not, under any circumstances, let anyone in besides my mother.

I know some of the crew are quite taken with you, but they might not be genuine."

"Espionage? Morse code?" These were her only questions. She knew how to protect herself.

"Deceit and spy work. Morse is a type of coded language that we use to communicate. All my friend will need to send back is a yes or no. I'll have to wait on the ship until that gets communicated back."

"Are you certain I shouldn't go back home with my parents? I would be safe there."

"As much as I entrust Mala and the rest of the group to oversee you, I worry that you going there would only give Ridgewell an excuse to head toward the inner land. You could unknowingly lead him right where he wants to be led. Right now, my mother is able to redirect him. Not for long. If there's evidence of tampering, we'll find a way to pull everyone off the project and leave you alone." He pushed the docked rowboat a short ways into the water with a pack of overnight things he took in a hurry from the tent.

"Please be safe! We can handle ourselves here." Thea ran a bit of the way into the water with him, nearly soaking her underthings in the process. She threw her arms around his neck, feeling the corded muscle on either side. She pressed her cheek into his chest out of fear that she may not see him again. Time used to feel like the only commodity she had on the island, and now she was running out of it. And fast.

John peered into her beautiful, vine-colored eyes, wanting to give her a solution he did not yet possess. All he could do was lean down, light brown hair framing his forehead and giving her a firm, but reassuring kiss. Nothing that would keep either of them lingering. But it was enough. Maybe.

"I'll do anything you ask," John finally replied, hiking his pants up as far as he could get them, jumping into the boat. "See you soon, Wild One." Jonathan pulled his arms back, landing the oars in still water, propelling them forward to start the short ride to the primary boat.

Thea focused on the mechanics of rowing, ignoring the jittering that racked through her body.

Thea didn't leave the shoreline until she was certain he was on the main ship. She squinted as dusk approached, and took in her surroundings.

The tent wasn't too far away, and Dr. Perch pushed her way out with a loud *flap* while holding a notebook. Thea gestured to where she was headed so Aggie would know where she would be, despite John's warning to stay by his mother's side.

"Don't be gone too long, my girl. We have much to discuss. And don't let anyone see you. I can only hold the staff off from looking for you for so long. Everyone's agenda is quite tight, and there's growing interest in your story."

Thea nodded, acknowledging the risk. She could only hope everyone else would do their part correctly. Aggie's distractions. The note getting sent back in a timely manner. Chase turning out to be someone more reasonable than she first encountered. But she was never very good at sitting still for long.

Vines were calling her name like a siren song. It was the only place she could think without repercussions. Just a few quick swings through the thick forest would be enough to ground her for the time being. She jogged into her jungle, her adopted home.

Thea used her long limbs to climb up the first thick, wooded tree she could find going all the way to the top. There, she took a few large deep breaths, wondering how anything could have gone this far. In a span of less than two weeks, she discovered her own identity and was developing feelings for a member of the opposite sex. Nothing she could have ever thought for herself. She certainly never thought that someone else would ever cater to her in such a way.

The air was thick in her lungs, and she decided to leap, one thick, corded vine in hand, already setting her sights on the next one to swing from. One jump, and Thea was back in it. She allowed herself a small smile when the wind whipped through her hair, the familiarity of it comforting. She approached the next tree, snagging up another vine just in time to keep up her momentum.

She contemplated what it would be like to head to the mainland. Maybe one of the Perches would allow her to live with them while she researched where she came from. She might have more relatives than her mother ever spoke of, or at least more than she remembered. If she could get a formal education at the same university her parents taught at, maybe she could start a true conservation effort on the island. Resources grew more scarce the older she got, but that wasn't something often discussed by Mala. Especially not the Boss.

Another vine approached. She caught it with ease.

Leaving her family would hurt, but what was best for her? Thea worked for the collective, never herself. She was an adult, and she wanted to explore a different kind of jungle. She decided the question wasn't in the if, it belonged in the how. There was time. There had to be. She'd discuss options with Aggie when she went back.

Another vine.

Another.

Another.

She needed to get back soon, but she heard voices where there shouldn't be voices.

What the hell is that sound?

Thea slowed down, swinging slower and slower until she was at a full stop. The vine she was currently occupying was low enough to nearly reach the ground, allowing her to slide down soundlessly. Undetected.

She reverted back to her roots, crouching on all fours, working her way toward the noise. She detected several men. Four, at the very least.

Thea knew she had to get close enough to hear the details of the conversation, because per the agreement, Chase and his cronies weren't supposed to be this far in. They were closer to the main gorilla encampment than they may have realized.

"I told that dirty bitch that I would be taking what I please. They just can't know about it yet."

"Yeah boss, these animals won't know what's coming to them."

"Yeah, yeah, we got our guns and ammo. What else could we need?"

"It's us versus them. Their pelts will be our profit very soon."

The collective laughter made her skin crawl. She creeped through the brush, trying to figure out what could have been going on. Pelts? For profit?

She had no weapon to her name, and there wasn't enough time to whittle anything down into something sharper. Thea didn't know much about modern weaponry, but she knew that guns could kill. Thea had little interest in being on the receiving end of one.

Chase's voice rang out against the crowd.

"Do you think these foolish primates will even know that we're here to hunt? No studying, just killing." He was rallying them. And quickly.

Thea attempted to process everything she was hearing. Her first interaction with him was him in his truest form, it seemed. She wasn't sure what to do first. Go back to Aggie? Stay and fight? Try to steal another boat and meet Jonathan on the main vessel? He'd be discovering Chase's intentions soon enough. And she wasn't supposed to wander too far from Aggie.

This was an absolute mess.

Going to Aggie would be the best idea. The safe idea. Going against her own instinct, she started to crawl backward. One painful step at a time, she was learning from the past. The ground was wet enough to not make much of a sound until she hit a puddle of water with a massive *squelch*.

Chapter 15

Thea's foot sunk deeper and deeper into the mud. It was sucking her limb down further and further. Her kneecap was nearly encapsulated within a minute.

No no no.

This couldn't be happening. If she made too much noise trying to pry her foot away, one of the men would notice. One, maybe two she could overpower. But not Ridgewell. Not the entire group. She only resorted to violence when she was stuck in a corner. And although not quite in a corner, she was most certainly stuck.

"Did anyone hear that?" One of the cronies said amongst the crew.

Laughter died down as the rest tried to listen.

"Just the wind."

"Maybe it was Jonsey's fart!"

Disgusting.

Thea slowed down her breathing, hoping to not create a disturbance. She looked around to see if a vine hung low enough near her. A quick scan around her showed that there was one within fingertip's reach. She stretched her long limbs as long as they possibly could have gone.

Slowly, painfully, she got her hand around the thick vine.

Come on. Just pull!

Her kneecap reemerged, and she was able to gain enough ground to wrap her other hand around the vine. Meanwhile, mugs were clinking and ale was sloshing. Conquering the island was something to celebrate, and they timed everything perfectly. One of the traitors must have overheard them plotting to get a message to the mainland, and started their journey into the jungle before dawn. Thea's muscles strained, burning with the counterpressure of the sludge.

One more pull, and she'd be up in a tree in no time.

"Well, well, well. What do we have here?"

Thea's heart fell into her stomach. She froze momentarily before continuing pulling herself out of it. Mr. Ridgewell loomed over her, distracting her progress. One haggard-looking older man was hacksawing away at the vine two feet from her hands. The last thread snapped, and her upper body fell back to the wet ground.

"Fuck you!" Thea spat out as she wiped her hand across her face to rid it of the wet dirt that was soon to dry on the side of her face. She used both hands to wrap around her calf, attempting to release her foot the rest of the way. "You're plotting to kill my family!"

"Fuck me? How about fuck you? You and your... monkey parents and siblings and whatever you call them. Fuck you and your stupid bitch of a mother!" He leaned down over her, spitting in her face. "Seize her immediately."

Thea got pulled the rest of the way out with zero finesse by the older guy and someone a little more spry. Their body odor made her eyes water worse than elephant droppings.

"Let me go! You are awful! You *smell* awful!" The goons held her tight, grabbing each one of her arms, surely to leave bruises. Self-defense strategy came to her since she luckily frequently grappled with her gorilla friends and family. She dropped as quickly as a stone tossed into a river, becoming dead weight. She yanked the two men down with her and kicked upward using both legs, one foot jamming into each jaw.

They let go with a cry and staggered away from her. She would show them the creature she had become. What the jungle shaped her into. She wasn't leaving without answers despite the guns from the rest of the crew, forming a semi-circle in front of her.

"My... My mother? Tell me. What does she have to do with this? She would never have sold herself out to kill and injure the inhabitants of this island." Thea started backing away, looking behind herself quickly enough to search the nearest vine for her to climb up and swing away. She had to get away, but didn't want to garner suspicion that she'd make a quick escape.

"I thought you would have figured it out by now. Always picking around our books. Learning how to read more eloquently. Even the pictures. Perhaps you haven't noticed." Ridgewell trailed off, almost speaking to himself for a moment.

"Your mother, Emilia—" he paused to spit on the ground as if to get her name off of his tongue, "She never did know what was the best for her."

"My mother?" Thea felt like the tape flailing at the end of the projector. "What did you know of her?"

"Know of her?" Ridgewell ground out. "We were together. Meant to be. She just didn't see it that way. Your meddling father had to come into our class and ruin it all. He ruined everything."

Thea's toes grappled with the ground for fear of falling over. This was it. He was in love with her mother and he was exacting his revenge.

"That ship was never supposed to reach the island." He stalked over to her quickly, closing all of the ground she covered. "You were never supposed to survive."

"You tampered with the ship? You hated my mother for not loving you so much that you wanted her and her family dead? With a newborn aboard? You're a sick, disgusting freak!"

Thea wanted to hear no further detail. She had to get her family evacuated. At the very least, she needed to gain back the ground she lost in this stand off. Thea started running backwards in order to get away.

The circle around her hadn't closed, and she started calling to her family. The signal was a primal yell with a particular cadence. It indicated one thing.

Danger.

"Get back here! Men! Chase after her!" The overwhelming stench of henchman nearly took her out on its own. The mechanical sounds of the gun machinery started to click into place. Thea heard a deafening shot, and a bullet pounded into a tree stump nearby.

Her bare, calloused feet pounded the ground, barely registering the pain of smaller twigs and bugs she was flattening in her wake. One bullet swiped at the long, dark hair flying behind her. Another close call.

The ground shook behind her, and she pumped her arms as fast as she could, propelling herself toward the nearest branch.

Ridgewell's large, grimy hands barely swept the bottom of her foot, and it would have tickled if it wasn't so intimidating. Luck was on her side, just barely, to show she was in a copse of trees perfect for swinging and dodging bullets. Manmade creations looked to destroy, but the trees were hers.

Gunshots followed her vine to vine.

Zia Tyree

CHAPTER 16

"Mala!" Thea cried. Her adoptive mother was the last one to leave the encampment. She must have been waiting for Thea. She dropped down from the last branch.

Child! Are you hurt? Mala hustled over to her daughter, using her large palms to assess Thea. She momentarily collapsed into Mala's awaiting arms, her body raging with adrenaline and coated in sweat. Thea was out of breath having swung with all of her might to make it back home. She didn't hide the mindspeak. Breath sawed out of her before she went for an explanation of the call to signal her family to flee.

"No, but you are all in incredible danger. The men. They're here for you. But not to study." Thea bent over, placing her hands against the tops of the thighs.

We have a moment. Take a breath, Wild One. You did so well. Mala rubbed Thea's back just like Emilia did when she was little. She took little comfort.

"They have guns. And Chase. Mr. Ridgewell? He was in love with my mother. So much so, that he sabotaged the ship. If he couldn't have her, he didn't want anyone else to either."

Don't worry about that now. I told The Boss to take off with the group. I knew you were coming, though, she pounded her chest. *I knew you'd want to make sure that we made it out. He nearly carried me out himself until I threatened him.*

Thea collapsed on the ground, her worn breast bandages feeling tighter than ever against the severe exertion. She hadn't thought to change into the normal clothes Aggie gifted her before she went swinging. They would have been much too restrictive.

You need to go with the rest of the pack until I can make sure you're safe. Please, hide, Thea begged.

I need to know that you are safe. Where is John? I need him to look after you. Mala's brow furrowed with concern.

"He's trying to get a message to the mainland. We wanted to know what Ridgewell's involvement was, and I discovered it the hard way. He has no idea that he and his terrible crew want to kill you and use you for... pelts." Thea had to speak it aloud to enhance the impact of her message.

Mala's eyes widened only for a moment before composing herself.

Now I know. Get back to the water. Get back to Jonathan. We will be okay. They don't know the island like we do. Mala leaned in conspiratorially before gently butting Thea. Forehead to forehead, Thea spoke into Mala's mind.

I love you. So much. And The Boss. Please tell him I love that stubborn, protective gorilla. Please know I will be okay. I will find a way to make sure the overseers of the project know the truth behind what's going on here.

I love you too, Wild One. Now go. For however long you may need. Mala motioned her palm over her own chest, and then put it over Thea's heart. *We will always be here.* Thea wasn't sure which one of them was more human at that moment. With a gentle push, Mala redirected the Thea back toward the water.

Onward, child.

Zia Tyree

CHAPTER 17

Thea approached the shore with hesitation. She didn't know who was a part of Ridgewell's secret mission, or who was just as oblivious as the Perches. Thea worked her way toward Aggie's tent as it wasn't too far from the treeline. She had left her there earlier this morning, and John should be back by now. Thea didn't care that she looked like death or that she was exhausted to her core. She just had to get back with safe people.

She pulled the tent flap to the side, seeing both Perches safe and together.

"Thea! Good god!" John ran over to her, embracing her tightly. He separated them briefly so he could assess her much like Mala did. "What happened? Where did you go?" He was frightened beyond belief. Less than two weeks they had known each other, and he was fretting over her constantly. He smoothed out her hair, bringing his hands on either side of her dirty face.

Thea grew breathless for a different reason.

Later.

"They're here to kill my family," she said without pretense. "Mr. Ridgewell was obsessed with my mother. To the point that he sunk the ship that brought her here. He never cared about the research. All he ever wanted was pelts. And money.”

Dr. Perch gasped. “That bastard. He must be involved with some sort of black market.”

“I’ll kill him! Where is he?” John’s eyes were bloodshot.

“No! You can’t! There are too many of them.” Thea put her head against his chest in an attempt to slow her racing heart.

“What did they do to you?” John’s voice went dark.

“I know I was meant to stay close, but the weather was perfect, and I got away from myself. I went swinging to clear my mind and went a little too far. I just had to. It’s when I clear my head the best. Anyway, I overheard him plotting with about five or six other men. Men I haven’t seen before. They’re out there right now, hunting my family. I signaled to them and they got away. I made it to our camp, and Mala stayed back to be the messenger. We have to do something."

"You'll want to hear what John discovered from his contact back home." Dr. Perch looked to the ground, crossed her arms and shook her head. "This is less than ideal."

"Less than ideal is putting it lightly. My contact said that he spoke with the archivist at the library. He said that Ridgewell wasn't in on the plans for that venture, but he convinced the Queen's counsel to fund it." John gripped the back of a chair so tightly that his usually tan knuckles went white.

"So that means that he really orchestrated it. The crew was smaller than normal, and the ship was incredibly sturdy. It would have easily managed any raging sea. The tampering must have been stealthy enough to have gone unnoticed by maintenance before departure, but strategic enough to collapse the ship in tumultuous waters." Dr. Perch went on, as she wrote down their findings in the journal she kept around, forever an erudite.

John remembered himself, stretching his neck to shake off the anger. He reached back for Thea. "I'm so sorry. We will make this right. As right as we can. For now, we need to get the hell out of here and come back with more resources."

"And abandon my family? Absolutely not." She pulled back from him, despite not wanting the distance. "We can't just 'get the hell out of here'. The fight has to come from us. You need to get back to the ship to get one more message out for help."

"We need to get back to the ship. I have to get you to safety." The pulse was beating out of John's neck. "He will kill you, Thea. Finish what he started. I can't let that happen. I'll kill him first." The violence and aggression wasn't something she had seen from John. It appealed to her animalistic instinct and she liked it.

CHAPTER 18

The trio snuck out of the tent as the sun was setting. The smell of fish cooked over charcoal wafted, and Thea's mouth watered. These people were colleagues to The Perches. They were laughing over textbooks and learning about coconut trees. It seemed harmless.

"Are we certain we can't trust anyone? I find it hard to believe that the students were interested in anything other than general island discovery." Thea wanted to believe the best in others, despite having poor beginnings with most of the humans she had encountered thusfar.

"Thea darling, I can hear your stomach from here. But I do see where you're coming from. What do you think, Mother?" Jonathan put a strong hand on his mother's shoulder.

"Even if we could trust the students, they don't have as much power as the ship hands to get us back to the mainland. We need to sneak some food from the storage, steal another small boat, and then manage to get back to the main ship to send a message," Dr. Perch said, fiddling with a pen.

"We stay stationary, hide on the ship, and wait for backup? Are we sure? It doesn't seem like enough." Thea had no tactical advantage, and she didn't want to waste time. Ridgewell could be coming upon her family at any moment, if they hadn't already. The gorillas would have stuck together, as a creature comfort, and the rest of the animal friends would have found a way to safely scatter. The devious sidequest wasn't after them, but one couldn't be too careful.

Thea hoped they got lost. Or managed to drown in a river. Or get bitten by one of the various snakes that inhabited the island. In any case, she wished them dead. She felt nothing else about the situation.

Thea volunteered to crawl on all fours in order to avoid being seen. At any point, the rest of the crew could seize them. She snagged a bag of bread, a bottle of something she learned was blackberry jam, and then some brown stuff that was sticky in its own right. It created one of her favorite sandwiches.

John stayed around the corner, gun in hand, serving as her backup should someone get too close. When Thea turned the corner back to John, they hurried to a secluded part of the beach where Aggie sat, hidden under brush.

"It won't be long until they come looking for me in my tent. They think I've been reading this entire time. It'll be odd that I haven't come out for dinner. They might get suspicious and realize we know what this mission is really about."

"Why bring us at all?" John was fixing the sandwich just like she liked—extra peanut butter. Tragic that there wasn't anything but a canteen of water to wash it down with. He held it out to Thea, a small smile on his face. She knew he wanted to offer more, but couldn't. "Why bring us if this was the plan the entire time?"

"What if the pelts weren't the only goal? What if there was something else?"

"Well, Chase was always upset over the grant," Dr. Perch whispered.

"The grant? What grant, Mother?" John finished making his own sandwich.

"Well, Nathaniel Underwood and Chase weren't just rivals when it came to your mother. They were rivals in every sense of the word. Academically, physically. Neither man was known to be disinclined to any activity. However, the only grant that Chase was ever granted that I've heard of was from the information we received today. Funding the Underwoods' exhibition to this island." Aggie chewed thoughtfully. "I just never thought... I never put the pieces together." Tears welled up in Aggie's eyes.

"Please. Don't blame yourself." Thea wrapped a hand around Aggie's. For someone so isolated, Thea felt lucky to be loved by the few women she had ever encountered.

"Thea, can we speak? Alone for a moment?"

"I would like a moment, too, actually. I need to review my notes. See if I missed anything." Dr. Perch furrowed her brow in consternation.

Thea allowed herself to be pulled deeper into the brush by the man who had become her lover, confidante, and friend.

"Come with me."

"I thought we already established I was coming with you."

She felt his palms sweat.

"You are extraordinary. You are everything I didn't realize I was looking for. Perfect, in every way for me. Come with me to my home. It could be our home. You can learn and grow in ways you hadn't ever thought possible."

Thea's throat dried. Leaving her family was a big ask, even though she all but got Mala's blessing. Was she ready to be among humans with their guns and weapons? At least her brand of chaos felt free.

"For how long? I don't know if I could stay away forever." Thea's heart beat rapidly, it must have been showing through her chest.

"I would never prohibit you from visiting this beautiful place! We could go back and forth at our leisure whenever it's safe to cross the water. Our research would be so advanced with your knowledge. Think about what we could bring back to the mainland. Together." Jonathan's eyes shone earnestly.

"And conservation efforts? We could protect my family so this will never happen again?" Thea crossed her arms around herself for comfort. The proposition was nearly too good to be true.

"We can figure everything out together, I just want you with me. We can have a life. Whatever that looks like." In the short time Thea knew John, he had never looked so unsure of himself. Maybe he expected less reluctance. She knew he didn't want to take her away from her home, but there was so much possibility across the water.

"Mala gave me her blessing. Earlier. When we were together. I think she wants me to find myself. I believe I can do that with you." The moonlight had never looked so beautiful shining against a face. The sun, the moon, every planet chose to illuminate him in just the right way. Blessed in some way. And she just... wasn't.

Jonathan wrapped her up in his warm embrace. His skin still smelled like the salt of the water and that comforted her. After a few deep inhales, the tension melted away. No matter what, they could get through it together. She couldn't help but feel like this was the type of love that her parents felt among each other.

He grabbed the tip of her chin, and tilted it toward himself.

"You are wanted. You deserve the world. Let me give it to you." With that, Jonathan placed his lips against hers in a tender yet heated kiss. She felt the familiar tingling in her bones whenever he was this close, touching her the way he did. Thea's instinct propelled itself to the surface, as she jumped on him, wrapping every limb around him like the green trees she knew so well.

John groaned against her lips, as his growing erection poked through his pants, suggesting something more against her core. He backpedaled against a tree, clearly needing to find some leverage. Thea chuckled softly under her breath. Every moment felt stolen, but she had no choice to get her hands on this man.

"Fuck, Thea. When you climb me like this, I just want to—" he took a deep, shuddering breath, stopping himself.

"What?" She said, placing small bites along the side of his neck. "What do you want to do to me?"

"You don't want to know. It's not very gentlemanly." His brow pulled together in frustration. With what, she didn't understand.

His hands were securely underneath her backside, keeping her as close to him as possible.

"I'm not a gentlewoman. I want to know. I deserve to know." Thea's voice dropped in pitch, seducing him on instinct.

"I want to fuck you against this tree. I want you to grab a vine in each hand, and drop straight onto my cock. But we can't do that. That's not right." He shut his eyes, not wanting to look at her. Was he embarrassed?

"Look at me. Don't you think I want that, too?" Thea's mother taught her to be in tune with her womanly cycle and prepared her for plenty when it came to this area of life, despite what John may have thought. "I'm not in the window of fertility. I would know." She continued her pursuit of sex, licking from the base of his neck all the way to his ear.

"Oh good god, don't tell me that. Please take that back." John turned them both around, pushing her up against the tree this time. He used one strong arm to keep her secured to him, and used the other to fondle her breast. He took her mouth deeply, sweeping his tongue against hers. He still tasted like peanut butter. She vaguely wondered if he cared that she did, too.

"I won't take it back. I need this. Something to recenter ourselves. We just have to be quiet," Thea said, hot breath scraping his ear.

"Oh, so you're the boss now? Telling me what to do?" John smiled against her lips.

He put her down momentarily, quickly looking around for a soft patch to lay in. The two scurried a ways deeper into the brush. Thea laid down first, taking off her underthings quickly. She was ready.

John let out a stuttering breath. "You are so beautiful. This is deeply irresponsible. But you are so... beautiful." He crawled over her, palming her sex. He sunk one thick finger into her heat, slipping in and out, much more quickly this time.

"You make me feel this way. Let's keep being irresponsible. Just for a few minutes, at least," Thea said, teasing him.

"Just wait until we're on the mainland. You'll be grateful if it's only for a few minutes at a time for what I'm planning to do to you." John pumped another finger in at that moment, drawing his fingers up with each stroke. He used his other hand to cover her mouth, knowing she'd make noise, willingly or not.

Her core built, clenching and preparing around his fingers. He thumbed her slickness, using it to circle her clit, and she exploded, bucking her hips against his entire hand working to bring her pleasure.

John's eyes darkened, and Thea caught up to her own breath.

"That was one, but I'm in the market for three."

John scooted down, clothes still on much to Thea's dismay, and pushed both of her thighs to her chest. His hot breath moved against her sex, tickling her inner thighs. With one long swipe, he licked her all the way to her sensitive bud. Her breath hitched at the boldness he exhibited in tasting her.

"I need you ready to take me. Your sweet cunt is the most delicious thing I've ever tasted. I'll never get enough of this." Those were John's final words before he mouth-fucked her pussy, capturing the bottom of the first orgasm, making it rise again and explode harder a second time.

This time, she had to clamp her own hand over her mouth to stifle the cry. It turned out that sex was an incredibly useful tool when it came to forgetting one's own problems.

Three was unconscionable. Thea was still pulsing when she was pulled back up to standing. He picked her back up, pushed her against a tree and placed a vine in each hand. What he said, he meant.

"I want you to hold on. You can control the pace. I want this to be good for you. As good as it can be." John looked around briefly to make sure they were still in a secluded-enough area, and stripped. His full manhood was glorious to see. Thea grew in wetness and attraction quickly. It was a miracle at this point that she possessed any upper body strength at all. She wrapped her hands around each vine a few times to give her some more leverage as he picked her up by her hips.

"Are you ready?" John said, brown eyes piercing her own. The biggest but most simple question.

"Yes." Thea nodded sharply, wanting to be close to him.

He teased her entrance, first slicking himself against her sex. She was so sensitive, but the need to come again was an imperative she couldn't ignore.

"Please, please, please," Thea begged. She lowered herself onto his cock before he got the chance to thrust up into her.

"Oh god, Thea. You feel so, so good. Work yourself onto me," John commanded.

She pulled herself up and down, up and down, working his cock. This was the most natural thing in the world, and it didn't hurt like she had been told. She was so aroused that she didn't notice anything outside of the delicious pressure she felt building back up into her core. John grabbed both of her hips and helped move her on his cock. Thea tossed her head back, realizing she needed this more than she had needed anything else. She was raised like an animal, and this was the clearest expression of that. She began to loosen her grip on the vines, her body becoming increasingly pliable against his touch. Soon his thrusts from underneath took over and she lost her grip on the vines. He tossed her hands around his neck for support.

"Hold onto me. Oh, yes, Wild One. Just like that. So good for me. You're a natural. At everything. I can feel you. I can feel you take me so well." The scent of his sex and sweat blended into a heady aroma. His words consumed her thoughts. She was doing well. Thea was so close.

"John, I—" she wasn't sure what she needed to finish this time. They were surely away from where they were supposed to be for too long.

John tilted his head and bit her breast, causing a mixture of pleasure and pain so extraordinary that Thea's third climax detonated, leaving her screaming into his shoulder. A few moments later, his hot come spilled inside of her, and he jerked until every drop was spilled. He gently pulled out and pulled her to him. He rubbed her back and kissed her softly without expectation of anything more.

Through heaving breaths and sticky skin, they found a small stream to wash up in. Thea felt more alive than ever before. More invigorated at taking on the mainland, despite what challenges may arise for them. She knew that if she could find family in gorillas, she could most certainly find family with the Perches. Maybe even get to make one of her own one day. John waded toward her, sinking to his knees, rinsing up and down her leg. He cupped the water, dripping it along her sex, washing away the evidence of what happened between them. She would have been sad for it, if his hands didn't swipe against her sex, still swollen and hungry. Thea was becoming insatiable.

"Think we'll be able to hide this from my mother?" John said, pulling her out of heat and reverie. "I might die if my mother knows that I have a sex life." John laughed softly.

"Must we hide?" Thea leaned down and trickled water over his head playfully. "After all, Aggie and your father had to have come together in a similar—"

"Oh good lord, please no. Not now. Not when I'm so happy and not grossed out." John chuckled, leading them out of the water.

"What we did was perfectly natural! Aggie is a woman. She will understand." Thea finished binding her breasts, put her hands on her hips, and started to stride toward the area they left Dr. Perch in.

CHAPTER 19

While John approached his mother sheepishly, Thea approached with full confidence. The confidence of a woman. She recently experienced a rite of passage, and she wasn't ashamed.

"Did we give you enough space, Dr. Perch?" Thea asked.

"I think the question should be, did I give you two enough space?" Aggie raised her eyebrows looking between the two of them. She stood up and brushed some remaining sand off of her cargo pants. "What next?"

The boat was easier to secure than they had thought. When John redocked earlier, he thought the ship hands that were stationed on the island brought it back to their makeshift port. But it remained near his mother's tent.

"The key will be to slip out on to the water without making too much of a splash," John whispered. They were covered in darkness now, and only a fire down the beachside and light of the full moon illuminated anything.

"How does one get into a boat? All I see is you men hopping into it."

Aggie, still clearly spry in her older age, demonstrated the art of getting inside, without stomping around.

"Your turn, my love. In you go." John held Thea's hand until she was safely inside the boat.

They reached the ship without being seen, and climbed up the side. John tied the boat down against the ship, and the boat tapped the ship's hull without contest.

He was last to come up, ensuring they weren't being followed from the shore and directed both women to the communication center of the ship. John urgently tapped away a message.

"Now would be a terrible time for the emergency receiver to be taking a break."

John explained earlier that general communication was meant for earlier in the day, and the line should only be used for emergencies at night. Clearly, this was an emergency.

He kept tapping out a distress signal. Nothing was happening. No one was coming.

"They have to respond quickly. What if the entire ship was in danger?" Dr. Perch piped up.

"Not if Larry is snoozing on the job. I'll never know why they moved him onto the night shift," John said.

"Move over, let me try something different," Aggie shooed her son off of the seat. She started pressing blue and white buttons and flipping red switches. Thea felt desperately useless.

"What are you doing? Can I help?" She began to wring her hands.

"Your presence is all that's required. You've had to fight for so long. We can take it from here."

She had to do something. "I'll be on the lookout for others. I'm still worried someone followed us."

"I don't want you out of my sight," John said.

"No squabbles. I'm trying to focus on finding another signal from the mainland. Maybe one that will actually follow through. John, hop on the other headset. I left the incoming signal open to multiple frequencies."

John obeyed his mother.

"I'm just going to take one quick peek! You won't even notice I'm gone!"

"Be quick about it! I don't want to be separated from you again!" John called after her.

Thea had to make herself useful, and she could use her eyes at the very least. She crept quietly around the corners of the ship. Some rumblings came from the bottom of the ship, but everyone who remained on the ship were in their sleeping quarters by now.

The wild woman found her way to the outside of the ship, peering over the railing. Taking in the ocean air felt different when she was actually on the water. The breeze was stronger, and the air was chillier. Now she regretted not accepting stronger outerwear. She walked softly to the other side of the ship's railing, ensuring her self-imposed lookout duties were being fulfilled.

She let herself close her eyes. She didn't feel the ship swaying too much in the water, but it felt familiar to the vines. Home was anywhere John was, she realized. They could curate moments that felt familiar and new at the same time. Even if it was on a top secret mission to rescue her gorilla pack family.

A strong hand grabbed her shoulder.

"Did someone get back to you?" Thea turned around with a calm smile until she was greeted by Chase Ridgewell.

"Expecting someone else?"

CHAPTER 20

"Get your fucking hands off of me!" Thea kicked and exclaimed. "JOHN. AGGIE. THEY'RE HERE!"

"I'm not letting you get away so easily this time," Chase said with malicious intent. "Grab those ropes. There! Yes!" His arm was around her throat this time, clamping down on her oxygen supply.

"JOHN! JOHN!" Her vision started to black out.

Fight. Fight like hell. She told herself.

With one swift buck, she knocked her head into his nose, immediately feeling the trickle of blood hot against her skin.

"Fuck! Be quiet!" He clamped his hand around her mouth, and she bit down on his ring finger, blood spilling in her mouth. Chase screamed in agony.

His cronies stood, frozen in place. They couldn't believe what they were seeing. She had clearly caused damage to them the first time around.

Chase dropped Thea, agonizing over his bleeding hand and nose. He looked like her worst nightmare. She scrambled away on all fours, never keeping her back to the band of abusers.

"HEY!" A loud gunshot rang through the air. John stood tall and proud, the gun still in his hand smoking. "Get away from her. Now." The promise of death was in his eyes.

The crew of bandits was seven deep, including Ridgewell. Three in total damaged one way or another. Only one had a gun on his person, but it was strapped against his back. Probably because he needed both hands to climb the side of the ship.

Good, Thea thought. Adrenaline spiked in her blood, and she could see even more clearly. The gun was poised directly at Chase's chest.

Chase put up his hands in mock surrender. "Come, now. We're all friends here. Aggie," he put a hand out with a fake plea.

"I told you. It's Dr. Perch, you sniveling, fake, arrogant piece of shit!" Aggie attempted to get in front of her son, but he nudged her back behind him.

"Hands up. And maybe I'll consider not shooting you." Thea knew John was lying. He was absolutely planning on gunning him down.

"This isn't what you think. Me and some of my colleagues here are just looking to get better acquainted with the gorillas. You understand, of course, that's what we're here to do."

"You're here for their pelts. You want them dead and sold to the highest bidder."

The gunshot had to have attracted everyone on the island whether they had been asleep or not. The trio would find out if they had allies soon enough.

"I'm here for... well. Several reasons." Chase turned on Thea, charging her, and tackling her to the ground. It happened too quickly for John to react. John opened fire on the crew who didn't scramble away of their own volition, and maimed several. John handed his gun to his mother, who had hardly any training, and jumped on Chase's back.

"Get! Off! Of her! Fight someone your own size, you jealous prick!" John pulled Chase off of Thea, and brought Chase to the ground, straddling him. Ridgewell just laughed.

"I had Emilia in a similar position once."

John pounded his face in. Over and over, blood coated the floor beneath them. Chase stopped moving. Thea tapped John out.

"John! John! It's over. He's out cold. He can't hurt us anymore."

Just as John pulled off of him and got a few feet away, Chase stood up, laughing all the way.

"Is that all you got?"

Chase tackled John to the ground, and the two men started rolling on the ship deck. Thea had to act fast. There was rope on the mast. She looked at Aggie and nodded toward it.

"Go! Quickly!" Aggie held the gun up, aimed at the ladder, the ship's main access point.

Thea climbed up the mast, not used to the slippery surface of metal. She would lose a foot of ground, but she persisted up and up until she grappled onto rope swaying from the top.

"John! Lookout!"

In an effort that might be their last, Thea leveraged herself, swinging straight for the two men. John saw at the last minute, and pushed Chase toward the railing. Chase's back was to Thea as she let out a wild scream.

"This is for my parents, you bastard!" Her feet collided with his chest, sending him flying over the rail, and straight into the water. Her momentum forced her to swing all the way around, hitting the ship deck running straight into John's arms.

"What's going on?" One of Dr. Perch's assistants said. The entire group of college students crept up the step ladder.

"Oh! Dr. Perch! Are you guys okay? We saw the extras leave on a skipper toward the mainland after we heard gunshots!" One of the female students explained. They couldn't have been a part of this. One threw up over the side of the railing at the sight of blood. They were clearly terrified of the bloodshed. It was all orchestrated by Ridgewell.

"Okay would be an interesting way of putting the past twelve hours," Dr. Perch said after letting out a long breath.

Zia Tyree

EPILOGUE

One year later...

"This is quite heavy. It might affect my grip," Thea said, holding her hand out, flailing it side to side, up and down.

"It's absolutely not heavy! You can take it off for exercise. And whatever else. I just want you to have it. It's nearly an exact replica of your mother's!"

"My mother was an incredibly practical woman. This is impractical. But very, very shiny. I'll keep it."

John let out a small huff. "How about I make your wedding band something simple and gold. You'll be able to wear it anytime, any place." He came around his newly-dubbed fiancée, overlooking the city on the terrace of the townhome he owned.

"That would be nice. And let's do it on the island."

"Get married? On the island? You can have whatever you want as long as you want to be my wife."

"That makes me so happy. Mala will be thrilled. Although I think I'll need to explain the human custom. The white gown and the cake. I do love cake. Does it come in peanut butter flavor?"

"No, but I'm sure we can get a layer of strawberry."

"Jam flavored. That will do," Thea held her hand out again, tilting her head to follow the sparkle in the dimming sun.

"Will you explain our silly human customs through your mindspeak again? The last time we visited the island, it was incredible to watch. I still have some questions about that, you know.

"Some things aren't meant to be researched." Thea put her hands through John's hair, savoring the softness through her own calloused fingers, and kissed him deeply.

Thank Yous

Thank you, from the bottom of my heart, to the local bookish community in Arizona. Without you, I would not be a part of such a fantastic group of writers and friends who help me learn and push the boundaries of my authorship on my first solo project. A very special thank you to Aly Hollis for bringing me onto the Flipped Fairytale project and for helping my novella dreams come true.

I also want to extend gratitude to my husband for believing in me, my work friends and family for supporting my continued passion in writing, and my Goalden Gals for holding me accountable every step of the way.

Also by Zia Tyree

The All's Fair Duet

All's Fair in Love and Construction

All's Fair in Love and Espresso

Stand Alones

Her Three Shadows

Flipped Fairytales

Tame Me Fiercely

part of a multi-author series

About the Author

Zia Tyree is a novelist and Registered Nurse. After spending countless hours devouring fantastical worlds and romance on pages, she decided to take matters into her own hands by crafting novels for other feisty romantics on her rare days off. When she's not writing, she's planning the next group get-together, sipping a coffee, or casting some sort of spell. She resides in the Southwest with her loving husband and three perfect rescue dogs.